The A26

The A26

Pascal Garnier

Translated from the French
by Melanie Florence

Gallic Books
London

This book is supported by the French Ministry of Foreign Affairs as part of the Burgess programme run by the Department of the French Embassy in London.

www.frenchbooknews.com

Liberté · Égalité · Fraternité
RÉPUBLIQUE FRANÇAISE

A Gallic Book

First published in France as *L'A26* by Zulma, 1999
Copyright © Zulma, 1999
English translation copyright © Gallic Books 2013

First published in Great Britain in 2013 by Gallic Books,
59 Ebury Street, London, SW1W 0NZ

A CIP record for this book is available from the British Library
ISBN 978-1-908313-16-4

Typeset in Caslon MT and American Typewriter by Gallic Books
Printed and bound by CPI Group (UK) Ltd, Croydon, CR0 4YY

For Isa and Chantal

The third streetlamp at the end of the road had suddenly gone out. Yolande closed her eye, which was pressed up to the shutter. The echo of the white light went on pulsing on her retina for a few seconds. When she opened her eye again there was only a black hole in the sky over the dead streetlamp.

'I've stared at it for too long, and the bulb's gone.' Yolande shuddered and left the window. She had been watching the street not through a gap in the shutter but through a hole made specially. In the entire house this was the only opening on the outside world. Depending on her mood, she called it the 'bellybutton' or the 'world's arsehole'.

Yolande could have been anywhere from twenty to seventy. She had the blurry texture and outlines of an old photograph. As if she were covered in a fine dust. Inside this wreck of an old woman there was a young girl. You would catch a glimpse of her sometimes in a way she had of sitting down, tugging her skirt over her knees, of running a hand through her hair, a surprisingly graceful movement in that wrinkled skin glove.

She had sat down at a table, an empty plate in front of her. Across the table another place was set. The ceiling lamp hung quite low, and was not strong enough to light up the rest of the dining room, which remained shrouded in darkness. You could sense, however, that it was cluttered with objects and pieces of furniture. All the air in the room seemed to be concentrated around the table, held within the cone of light shed by the lampshade. Yolande waited, bolt upright in her chair.

'I saw the school bus this morning. The children were wearing every colour imaginable. Getting off the bus, they were like sweets spilling out of a bag. No, it wasn't this morning, it was yesterday, or maybe the day before. They really did look like sweets. It brightened up just then, a streak of blue between the clouds. In my day children weren't dressed like that. You didn't get all those fluorescent colours then, not anywhere. What else did I see? Any cars? Not many. Oh yes, there was the butcher this morning. I'm sure it was this morning. He comes every Sunday morning. I saw him parking, the old bastard. He's always trying to see in. He's been at it for years. He never sees anything, and he knows he never will.'

Beef, some stringy, some covered in fat, with a marrow bone to boil up for a *pot-au-feu*. It was ready, had been cooking away all day. *Bub, bub, bubble.* The pan lid was lifting, dribbling out greyish froth, a powerful smell, strong like sweat. 'What else did I see?'

Yolande showed no surprise at hearing the three quick taps at the door and the key turning in the lock. Her brother had always knocked three times to let her know it was him. There was no point, since no one ever came. But he did it anyway.

Yolande was still sitting with an empty plate. The room was cold, the cooker was off. Bernard hung up his wet coat. Underneath he was wearing an SNCF uniform; he worked for the railways. He was around fifty, and looked like the sort of person you would ask for some small change, the time or directions in the street. He greeted his sister with a kiss on the back of the neck as he went round to take his place opposite her. Locking his fingers, he cracked his knuckles before unfolding his napkin. He had a yellowish complexion and big dark shadows under his eyes. His flattened hair showed the circular imprint of his cap.

'Haven't you started? You should have, it's late.'

'No, I was waiting for you. I was wondering when the school bus last went by.'

'Saturday morning, I expect.'

'You've got mud all over you. Is it raining?'

'Yes.'

'Oh.'

They were both equally still, sitting upright in their chairs. They looked at each other without really seeing, asked questions without waiting for an answer.

'I had a puncture coming home from the station, near the building site. It's all churned up round there. You'd think the earth was spewing up mud. That's their machinery, excavators, rollers, all that stuff. The work's coming along quickly, but it's creating havoc.'

'Have you still got a temperature?'

'Sometimes, but it passes. I'm taking the tablets the doctor gave me. I'm a bit tired, that's all.'

'Shall I serve up?'

'If you like.'

Yolande took his plate and disappeared into the shadows. The ladle clanged against the side of the pot, and there was a sound of trickling juices. Yolande came back and handed the plate to Bernard. He took it, Yolande held on.

'Have you been scared?'

Bernard looked away and gave the plate a gentle tug.

'Yes, but it didn't last. Give it here, I'm feeling better now.'

Yolande went back for her own food. From the shadows she said, without knowing whether it was a question or a statement, 'You'll get more and more scared.'

Bernard began to eat, mechanically.

'That may be, I don't know. Machon's given me some new pills.'

Yolande ate in the same way, as if scooping water out of a boat.

'I saw the butcher this morning. He tried to see in again.'

Bernard shrugged. 'He can't see anything.'

'No, he can't see anything.'

Then they stopped talking and finished their lukewarm *pot-au-feu*.

Through the closed shutters, shafts of light came in from the street, illuminating the chaos cluttering the dining room. A network of narrow passages tunnelled through the heaped-up jumble of furniture, books, clothing, all kinds of things, made it possible to get from one room to another provided you walked like an Egyptian. Stacks of newspapers and magazines just about managed to prop up this rubbish tip, which threatened to collapse at any moment.

At the table, Yolande had swept the used plates, cutlery and glasses from the evening before over to one corner. She was busy cutting pictures out of a magazine and sticking them on to pieces of cardboard to make a kind of jigsaw puzzle. By day the pendant lamp still oozed the same dead light as it did by night.

'Bernard's not gone to work today, he wasn't up to it. He's getting tireder and tireder, thinner and thinner. His body's like this house, coming apart at the seams. Where am I going to put him when he's dead? There's not a bit of space left anywhere. We'll get by, we've always got by, ever since I can remember. Nothing has ever left this house, even the toilet's blocked up. We keep everything. Some day, we won't need anything else, it'll all be here, for ever.'

Yolande hummed to herself, to the accompaniment of mice scrabbling and Bernard's laboured breathing in the room next door.

He was asleep or pretending to be. He was fiddling with a sparkling pendant on a gilt chain: 'More than yesterday and much less than tomorrow.' He wouldn't be going back to the doctor's. Even before setting foot in the consulting room he had known it was his final visit, almost a matter of courtesy. As usual, Machon had adopted specially for him the jovial manner which he found so irritating. But yesterday evening he'd struck more false notes than usual, stumbling over his words while looking in vain for the prompt. In short, when he'd sent Bernard away, his eyes had belied what his lips were saying.

'It's a question of attitude, Monsieur Bonnet, and of willpower. You've got to fight, and keep on fighting. In any case, you'll see, two or three days from now and you'll be feeling much better. Don't forget now, take three in the morning, three at lunch time and three in the evening.'

It was true, on leaving Bernard had felt relief, but that had had nothing to do with the medication. These regular appointments with the doctor, for months now, had been eating away at him as much as his illness, a never-ending chore. He who had never been ill in his life had experienced something like profound humiliation at handing himself over body and soul to Dr Machon, despite knowing him well. Every Wednesday for years now, the doctor had caught the train to Lille to see his mother. They had ended up exchanging greetings and passing the time of day until there had grown up between them not a friendship exactly, but a very pleasant acquaintanceship. As soon as he'd begun to feel ill Bernard had quite naturally turned to him. He'd soon regretted it, he had become his patient. In front of the large Empire-style desk he'd always felt like a suspect stripped for questioning, one of life's miscreants. These days whenever he met the doctor at the station he felt naked in front of him, completely at a loss.

Bernard had crumpled up the prescription and got behind the wheel of his car. There had been no puncture beside the building site.

Spurts of water added whiskers to each side of his Renault 5. Bernard was discovering life in its tiniest forms. It was there, rounding out with yellow light each of the droplets of rain starring the windscreen, million upon million of miniature light bulbs to illuminate so long a night. It was there too in the vibrations of the steering wheel in his hands, and in the dance of the windscreen wipers, which reminded him of the finale of a musical comedy. The anguish of doubt gave way to the strange nirvana of certainty. It was a matter of weeks, days, then. He had known for ages that he was dying, of course, but this evening he felt he had crossed a line. Deep down, these last months, it was hope which had made him suffer

the most. 'Bernard Bonnet, your appeal has been refused.'
He felt liberated, he had nothing more to lose.

Then in the beam of the headlamps, he had seen the
redhead, thumbing a lift, caught in a mesh of rain and dark.

'What an awful night!'

'Three months at the most,' he had thought. She smelt
of wet dog. She wasn't even twenty, surely.

'I've missed the bus to Brissy. Are you going that way?'

'I'm going nearby, I can drop you off there.'

She had a big nose, big bust and big thighs and smelt of
wide open spaces, the impetuousness of youth. Bernard's
uniform must have made her feel safe, as she was making
herself at home, undoing her parka and shaking out her
mop of red hair.

'The next one's not for half an hour, and I don't want to
wait. I'll be eighteen in a month, and sitting my test. I've
been saving up, and for a car as well. My brother-in-law's
going to sell me his – it's a Renault 5, like yours.'

'That's nice.'

'Don't I know you? D'you work at the station?'

'Yes.'

The stripes on her trousers looked like scratches. She
had sturdy thighs, and the same smell as Yolande when
she came home late from the factory. Their father would
thump his fist on the table.

'Have you seen the time?'

'Well, how d'you expect me to get home? There isn't a
bus any more. There's a war on, haven't you heard? What
are we having to eat?'

They always had the same, and she would always have
some boyfriend waiting in the wings.

'Why are you smiling?'

'Because you remind me of my sister when she was your age.'

'Oh. What's she called, your sister?'

'Yolande.'

'I'm Maryse. And what about you, what's your name?'

'Bernard.'

'Like my brother-in-law!'

She was practically family. Nothing for it but … He had stopped thinking about his death. This girl was like his life, a huge gift which he hadn't dared even begin to unwrap.

'What does your sister do?'

'Nothing.'

'Housewife and mother, then?'

'Something like that.'

On each side of the road the houses dissolved in a wash of brown ink. A triangular yellow sign had appeared right in the middle of the road, forcing a diversion.

'The fucking motorway, it's driving me mad! We don't need it, do we?'

'The march of progress. If you'll excuse me, I just have to stop for a few minutes, a call of —'

'Got it!'

The girl's laughter had sounded in his ear like the tinkling of the doorbell when you're not expecting a visitor. The rain had eased off and was now little more than a drizzle, the tears of a star freshening his face. Standing squarely in the mud, he had urinated against a concrete block bristling with metal rods. Work on the motorway had begun at the same time as his pain. With a wry smile, he noted how fast it was progressing. The arched back of the unfinished A26 soared like a diving board into the violet sky. A star had appeared between two banks of cloud. His hard-on was so big that he hadn't been able to do up his flies again. On the way back to the car his feet made a squelching sound with every step.

'I'm sorry, I've dropped my watch. There's a torch in the glove compartment.'

'Would you like some help?'

'That would be good. Thank you.'

The pair of them had waded about in the mud, Maryse's backside just a few centimetres from Bernard's nose. A whole life right in front of him. The girl had made a sound like a deflating balloon when he had jumped on her. Lying on top of her wildly flailing body, he held her head down in a puddle. It had gone on for quite some time, the girl was sturdy. But the grip of Bernard's hand on the back of her neck had finally proved too much for Maryse's 'nearly' eighteen years. 'Strong as death! I'm as strong as death!' His eyes were like a hound's when it bays at the moon. The water in the puddle became calm again. Soon it reflected nothing but a sky empty save for one quivering star. Bernard had loosened his grip. A slender gilt chain had got twisted round his wrist, at its end a small disc inscribed 'More than yesterday and much less than tomorrow'.

The hardest part had been dragging her to the far side of the building site. There he had heaved the body into one of the holes which would be filled in with vast quantities of concrete the next day, and covered her with earth. Maryse no longer existed, had never existed perhaps.

Bernard let the chain drop back on to his belly. It was unbelievably heavy. He thought he would give it to Yolande as a present. What would become of her without him? Nothing. She had stopped 'becoming' the best part of fifty years ago.

She would go on, every morning knitting the little scrap of life which she then unravelled every night, tirelessly, without ever thinking there might be an end.

'Bernard, there's the grocer's van!'

'I'm tired, Yoyo. Do you really need something?'

'Yes! Those little chocolate biscuits with the animals on. Please …'

'OK. Give me my coat, will you?'

'Get a few packets, just in case.'

Since Monday evening there has been no news of young Maryse L., born on 4 April 1975 in Brissy. The young woman was last seen close to the Jean-Jaurès bus stop. She is described as one metre sixty-four centimetres tall, of medium build, etc. Anyone with information should contact the police in ...

Bernard did not think the photo was a good likeness.

Newspaper photos never looked like anything, or rather they all looked alike, sharing a family resemblance, hangdog and miserable. The papers said any old thing. They never had anything very interesting to report, so they told lies. There wasn't so much as two lines to be said about the girl. Apart from a handful of individuals, no one knew Maryse existed. Her death made no difference. What album had they dug that photo out of? She couldn't be more than twelve in it. The silly smile of the young girl turned his stomach.

'Oh Bernard, you haven't eaten a thing! That's no good, and you know you like shepherd's pie.'

'I have, Jacqueline, I've had some. I'm just a bit out of sorts, that's all.'

'I can see that. You haven't touched your food. Have you seen Machon again?'

'Yes, on Monday. Everything's fine.'

'Everything's fine, my foot!'

Jacqueline put her pile of plates down on the corner of the table and ran her hand over her face as if removing an invisible spider's web. She had had this habit ever since they'd been at primary school together. Jacqueline was his best friend. They might have got married, had children, a dog, a caravan, the most modest of lives but a life even so. But there was Yolande. Jacqueline had waited for a long time, and then married Roland. They had the restaurant across from the station.

'Are you coming on Sunday, for Serge's First Communion?'

'I don't know, maybe.'

'But you've got to. He'd be hurt … I suppose you're fretting about Yolande, is that it?'

'Of course not.'

'Of course you are! She'll take advantage of you for your whole life, that one! Why don't you put her in a home? It's about time you started taking care of yourself. Have you looked in a mirror recently?'

'You know perfectly well that's impossible. She's not capable of —'

'Give me a light, will you? Yes, Roland, I'm coming, just a second! He's a bloody nuisance, that one. Can't do a damn thing for himself. It's a mess, isn't it?'

'Please don't start, Jacqueline.'

'What? What would we have left if we no longer had our regrets?'

'Remorse, perhaps.'

'Sometimes I think I might prefer that. At least it would mean we'd done things.'

'Things? They don't leave much of a trace behind them.'

'Well, did you want to leave pyramids behind you? Things aren't just stuff made of stone, your churches, castles, monuments! It's the little things, like when you used to go fishing in bomb craters, smoking your first cheap cigarette round the back of the bike sheds, all the things we said we were going to do even if we already knew we'd never do them … I'll be right there, I said! Please come on Sunday, just for me.'

'All right, I'll be there.'

Jacqueline got up with a sigh. She could almost have supported the tray on her ample bosom, leaving her hands free to carry other plates, other dishes. It must feel good to lie sleeping on those breasts, like being on a cloud. A long time past, down by the canal, the weather was hot. You could smell fresh grass. He had laid his cheek on Jacqueline's white breast. Beneath the thin stuff of her blouse he could feel her quivering, giving off a fragrant dew. Fish were jumping, snapping at dragonflies. The air was alive with a thousand tiny things. One of them had said, 'This is nice, isn't it?'

*

The small fluorescent green letters on the screen were no longer making proper words. They were now just long wiggly caterpillars, line upon line of them.

'Is something wrong, Bernard?'

'No, a spot of dizziness, that's all. It must be the new pills. Take over from me, François. I'm just nipping out for a breath of air.'

'Of course. Why don't you take some time off?'

'I'll think about it.'

Where did those rails along the platforms go? Not all that far. They joined up again over there, behind the warehouses, the end of the world was within arm's reach. Everything was rusty here, down to the ballast stones, even the grass clinging to life beside the track. The railway had left its mark, a lengthy scar with dried blood at the edges. Sitting on a trolley, Bernard ran his fingers over his face, feeling the rows of teeth, the angle of the jaw. Beneath the pallid, soft skin a death's head was hiding, like the one on a pirate flag or the labels of particular bottles at the pharmacy, with two crossbones behind. So what if it was ugly here, it was still the richest landscape on earth. You could make a life here. It was all there ahead of him, rails leading to more rails, on and on to infinity. François was right, he would take some leave. Actually, he would leave. Like old Fernand the year before. But he'd been retiring. He was old. He had gone off with a fishing rod under his arm, a cuckoo clock and a return ticket to Arcachon, first class. Bernard would never go to Arcachon. To tell the truth, he didn't give two hoots about Arcachon, there were so many places in the world where one would never set foot.

What was there, anyway? A dune, a big Dune of Pilat which looked just like the desert, they said. It was people who'd never been there who said that. Everything looked like everything else, people couldn't help comparing the things they knew to the things they didn't know, so they could say they did know, that they'd been round the world without leaving their armchair. Six of one and half a dozen of the other, no cause for regrets. No gifts for sick employees, they'd prefer them just to clear off, preferably without a trace. Illness really annoyed them, it was bad for business, and they took a dim view of it. It lowered the troops' morale.

'Oh my poor Bonnet, and with your poor sister too! How much time off do you want?'

Taking his cap between thumb and forefinger, Bernard sent it flying somewhere over the containers, like a Frisbee. He had another one in the locker room. No harm done. The wind caressed his baldness. In the early days, when Yolande's hair had begun to grow back he'd loved running his hand over her head. All the little hairs standing upright had given him a feeling like electricity in his palm. Her hair had grown back pure white. Yet she was only twenty. The shock of it, no doubt. Before that it was blonde, red blonde, Titian she used to call it.

WITH SEVEN CENTIMETRES OF HAIR
I have already told you how hard-working the Germans are. They make clothes and chocolate out of wood, and make lots of things from all sorts of materials which have not been used until now. They have now discovered

it is possible to make felt hats out of the hair cut off by the hairdresser. It is likewise possible to make rugs from these hair clippings. Since hair has to be a certain length for this, however, people are not allowed to have it cut before it reaches this length. If the hairdressers are diligent and collect up the hair carefully, in one year almost 300,000 kilos of hair will be obtained. That sounds like a lot of hats and quite a few rugs.

There it was in black and white, in the girls' own annual *La Semaine de Suzette*, under the heading 'Suzette across the world', an old copy from 1932, worn to a shine, stained and yellowing, like everything from that era. Despite knowing it by heart, Yolande loved to spend hours leafing through it. She had done all the crosswords, every rebus and sewn the entire wardrobe for Bleuette (a 29-centimetre doll with real curled hair, eyes that shut, and unbreakable posable head). She loved the smell it gave off when the pages were opened, a musty smell of old biscuits. The Germans would be back. She wasn't especially waiting for them but she knew they'd be back.

It was the drop of water falling on her newly shaven head which had hurt her the most, a deafening sound like the stroke of a gong which had stayed with her ever since. As for everything else, she had let them get on with it, like a sheep, there was nothing else to be done with morons like that. For as long as they kept her in the café, amidst their yelling, she had been outside her body. She was a past master at switching off, what with her bastard of a father who would bawl her out for the slightest thing. She'd had enough time to practise. But on leaving the Café de la

Gare, after they'd let her go, *plop!*, a large drop filled with all the absurdities of the past four years. It was as though the sky had been holding itself back ever since they'd dragged her out of her house, so as to fall in on her with all its might in that drop.

Yolande didn't even remember the Boche's name. To tell the truth, it wasn't so much for what she'd done with him that they'd shaved her head, more for what she'd refused to do with some of her 'barbers'.

What did it matter anyway? She had never liked them, they had never liked her. It had let her get shot of the damned lot of them once and for all. Besides, they must all be dead by now. But what had he been playing at in the lav for the past hour?

'Bernard, what are you doing in there?'

'Trying to unblock the toilet. How many times have I told you not to use newspaper!'

'I didn't have anything else. You forgot to get bog roll when you were at Auchan.'

'There's tissues.'

'They're no use to me, there's nothing to read on them.'

The sound of the flush drowned out Bernard's reply. He emerged from the toilet, wiping his hands. He was wearing a white shirt, the collar gaping wide round his thin neck.

'What are you dressed up like that for? Are you going to a wedding?'

'No, it's Jacqueline's nephew's First Communion. I told you that last night.'

'You didn't tell me a thing. You're always up to something behind my back.'

'For one thing, I did tell you, and for another, I'm not up

to anything. I'm going to the Communion, that's all.'

'So basically you're going to get sloshed and let her sucker of a husband foot the bill.'

'Yoyo, that's enough. I won't be staying long. I'm done in but I've got no choice. I won't be late back. The toilet's unblocked and I'm begging you, please don't put any more newspaper in there.'

Yolande shrugged and buried herself in *La Semaine de Suzette* again. Bernard rolled down his sleeves, slipped on his jacket and planted a kiss on his sister's neck.

'Come on now, don't sulk – I've got a present for you.'

The pendant on its gilt chain was dangling over the annual like a pendulum. Catlike, Yolande caught at it.

'What does that mean, "More than yesterday and much less than tomorrow"? Is it about the blocked toilet?'

'No, it means I love you more than yesterday and much less than tomorrow.'

'You're going to love me less tomorrow?'

'No, it's the other way round.'

'It's beyond me. Can you put it on for me?'

Bernard's fingers fumbled with the clasp. Strange, the skin on Yolande's neck wasn't an old lady's but a baby's, all soft, warm little folds.

'You're very beautiful.'

Yolande put the pendant into her mouth.

'I used to have one with the Virgin Mary, a blue one, it tasted of electric wire. At school when you went for an X-ray, you had to put it in your mouth so they didn't see the Virgin Mary in your bones. This one doesn't taste of anything.'

'See you later, Yolande.'

The countryside, accustomed to low skies and drizzle, looked ill at ease in its Sunday best in the sunlight. The bricks were too red, the sky too blue, the grass too green. It was as if Nature felt embarrassed at being so extravagantly made up. She was quite still, as if for the camera, except for the occasional crow hopping about in the middle of a field. At the wheel of his car Bernard was feeling good, for the first time in a long while. He loved these expanses of brown stretching as far as the eye could see, you could almost fancy you were by the sea. He passed a motorcyclist at the roadside, leaning against his bike. He was smoking a cigarette, at right angles to the line of the horizon. There was no house nearby. Here was a chap who had simply said to himself, 'I know what, I'll stop here for a cigarette because this is absolutely the best place in the world for that.' It was over in seconds, just the time it took for the motorcyclist's image to disappear in the rear-view mirror, but Bernard felt every bit of that man's happiness in his own body: 'I feel good.'

'And what about me? What will become of me while Yolande's still here?' He realised he had never asked himself that question before. He would very much have liked to be a biker stopped at the roadside for eternity. No doubt Yolande had never asked herself that question either.

She didn't care, had never cared about anything but herself. It couldn't really be called egotism, she had simply never been aware of other people. They were bit parts, at most, even her brother. When she had come home with her head shaven, never to leave the house again, she had appeared relieved, her face serene like that of a young nun. They didn't want her any more, and she had never wanted them. At last things were clear, ordered, everyone in their place. She had never wanted anything but this cat's life of cosseting and food.

Bernard slowed down as he passed the works on the A26. The pillars supporting the slip road had advanced a few steps. RIP Maryse.

'Now, Bernard, that's not an empty glass, is it?'

'Yes, but I'm fine, thanks.'

Roland's eyes looked like two blobs of phlegm, pastis yellow shot through with red.

'It's lovely to see the young ones having fun, so full of life!'

In the back room of the café, where the tables had been arranged in a horseshoe, the young ones were jigging to one of the summer's hits. The acrylic of the girls' little skirts was stretched out of shape over their bulging thighs. The boys, a glint in their eye, were blowing themselves a smoke screen to hide their acne and drinking out of cans. Jacqueline, hair dishevelled, was zigzagging amongst the dancers with a tray in her outstretched hand. She looked like a statue carrying its upturned plinth.

'She's not bad, even now, huh?'

'No.'

'Even with a few miles on the clock she's still a catch, don't you think?'

'Yes.'

'I'm telling you, Bernard, not only am I not angry with you, I feel sorry for you. Yes, I do, don't argue. What's more, out of all the men who've come sniffing around after her, you're the one I like best. You are! Because you're going to kick the bucket soon – before me. Not by much maybe, but before me.'

Roland's brow was dripping with sweat. The few hairs he had left were plastered to his temples. He'd been a very good footballer, the best goalkeeper Subligny had ever had, and had inherited the café-restaurant from his parents.

'I had to tell you, Bernard – it may not seem like it but I respect you. Look, if you want to, you can have her right here and now, before my very eyes, and I won't say a thing. Scout's honour.'

'You're talking rubbish, Roland. You're drunk.'

'Not at all! You'll see. Jacqueline! Hey, Jacqueline!'

'What's the matter with you? You must be out of your mind, yelling like that!'

'He won't believe I respect him! Do your business, you two, and I won't so much as raise my little finger. Go on!'

'You must be mad! There are children present!'

'So, there's children. They've got to learn the facts of life, haven't they? Like on the farm, the pigs with the sows, and the mares with the … I don't know what, but that's nature's way, isn't it, shit!'

'Be quiet! It's you who's the pig – clear off, you're ruining it all.'

The music had stopped, and so had the dancers. Some of them were sniggering behind their hands, others rolled their eyes. Only Serge, whose Communion they were celebrating, still moved around between them on his brand-new rollerblades.

'I've got to go, Jacqueline.'

'No, you don't, that's stupid.'

'It doesn't matter. It's not because of him, I'm just tired. I was leaving anyway. Say goodbye to Serge from me.'

Out in the car park Bernard rubbed his eyes. The red sphere of the setting sun was pulsing on his retina. Someone knocked on the window.

'Hello. Which direction are you going?'

The girl was made up like someone from a silent film, hair all over the place, black and red, like a kid disguised as a witch.

'Towards Arras, but I'm turning off in six kilometres.'

'That'll still be a help. Could you give me a lift?'

'If you like.'

She was wearing such a lot of heavy perfume, she needn't have bothered getting dressed.

'On Sundays, the buses ... Is it all right if I smoke?'

'Of course.'

The girl lit a cigarette. The smoke lingered above their heads. They weren't saying anything. Bernard was driving slowly. The sky took on streaks of purple and mauve.

'It's pretty. All this silence does you good.'

'Yes, it's like staring into a fire in the grate.'

'Wasn't there a war here?'

'That's right. The Great War and the other one. It's taken a while for it to look alive again.'

'Do you remember the war?'

'Just a little. I was young then.'

'All our lives we've heard people talking about it on TV, all over the world, but we can't really take it in. We're not quite sure it exists. It's like fairytale monsters, and ogres and death. We know it exists but we don't believe in it. We doubt everything, even ourselves. We're never quite sure we're not in a video game.'

'Does that bother you?'

'No, you just have to get used to it. I spotted you just now during the shouting match. You were different from the others. Me too. I'd come with a mate of the boyfriend of ... well, whatever, it's a shame, he was cute. You look so sad ... it's nice.'

'I'm not sad.'

'You look it.'

The sound the girl's stockings made as she crossed her legs caused him to jerk the wheel. But he was very swiftly back in control. She had noticed. He could just imagine the smile on her face as she crushed her cigarette end in the ashtray.

'What do you do for a living?'

'I'm going to drop you off here.'

'Really?'

'Really.'

Bernard parked on the verge. A car hooted as it went by. The lower part of the sky was turquoise with a tinge of gold right at the top.

'OK, well, thanks a lot anyway.'

'What's your name?'

'Vanessa.'

'Goodbye, Vanessa. Very nice to have met you.'

Vanessa, the motorcyclist, Jacqueline, all of them in the rear-view mirror, in one small piece of mirror which saw things back to front. A life wasn't very much, not much at all. Giving, taking away. It was so easy. Sometimes death spares people.

Yolande was making pancakes, dozens of them, building them up into an enormous stack. There were enough to feed at least fifty. It was her only way of combating the successive waves of 'outside' which had been beating against the walls of the house non-stop since the morning. For almost two hours now she had been busy, frying pan in hand at the stove. To begin with, she had counted them, as people count sheep to fall asleep, but then it had become mechanical, like breathing: a ladle of batter, turn the pan, wait, toss the pancake, wait, put it on the pile, a ladle of batter, turn the pan … They were like the skin of faces, faces she could put names to: Lyse, Fernand, Camille … She saw them go past one after the other, the way they used to lean over her cradle, gigantic, stinking of beer or cheap perfume, and belching out their slobbering coochie-coos, disgusting. Even then she had hated them, was nothing to do with them. She had only had to look at her father's face or her mother's belly to know for certain that she did not come from 'that'. Each time she tossed a pancake bubbling with dark craters, she said, 'Nice one.'

An hour after Bernard had gone out, the clock-radio in his room had come on by itself: 'Stock market news now, and all week the CAC 40 has been on a continual ...' Yolande had jumped in her chair. She had been in the middle of copying a map of France, concentrating, tongue sticking out, on making a good job of the shades of blue along the coast with a coloured pencil.

'Who's that? Who's there?'

She had taken the poker from where it hung on the handle of the stove and burst into Bernard's room, brandishing it aloft. The metallic voice coming from the small plastic box by the unmade bed had metamorphosed into an unbearable loud rasping with the first blow of the poker. But the creature was not dead and Yolande had had to finish it off with her heel to silence it for good. It had been some time before her nerves recovered and she was able to pick up her pencil again to draw the outline of Finistère.

The 'nose of France' was so hard to manage, with all the little ins and outs of the coastline from Saint-Brieuc to Vannes. She had always got ten out of ten for her maps; they would be pinned up in the classroom they were so beautiful. For that she'd needed to sharpen her coloured pencils really well and wet their points with spit. It was Brittany Yolande took the greatest pains over, because of the holidays. There were cousins in Pénerf, a little village near Vannes. Yolande used to have a thin frock in embroidered muslin from St Gallen, with tulle trim at the shoulders and waist, and a sky-blue straw cloche hat. But most of the time she would be in her bathing suit, barefoot, spattered with sand up to her knees. Every day, crowds of workers would pour out of excursion trains for their first visit to the seaside. Only the villa residents held themselves aloof from this display of overwhelming joy. It seemed as if the holidays would never end, like the Paradise they learnt about at First Communion classes. Yolande had a constant humming in her head. Perhaps it was from pressing seashells to her ear, or maybe the water from all the swimming. Yannick had white-blond hair, dry as straw. They would have play fights with sticky seaweed, and, squealing wildly, feel for each other with outstretched arms, under cover of the foam. That was the first time she had kissed using her tongue. For everything it was the first time.

A thudding at the door had ripped through the iridescent haze of her holidays at Pénerf. Her pencil point had snapped clean off on the south of Brittany. Yolande had pressed her eye up to the world's arsehole; two women, one stout and the other small, were rummaging in the letter box. They had waited, while Yolande held her breath. She had rumbled them, they were Boches disguised as French. Unless they were the girls from the Resistance done up to look like Boches ... You could never tell, there was no difference. Either way, playing dead was the thing if you wanted to stay alive. The two women had taken a step back and then moved off. Yolande had waited for a long time before retrieving the piece of paper from the letter box: 'Do you know the Bible?' Yolande hadn't read to the end of the text because it was obviously written in code, the proof being that it was signed 'The Jehovah's Witnesses'. What a bunch of losers! There would never be witnesses at her trial, because there would never be a trial. Bernard had promised her that. But they kept on trying all the same; they needed guilty people, even guilty people who were innocent, to fuel their morbid obsession with stamping out clandestine goings-on. That being so, she had to be on her guard; they would be back, they always were. That was her day shot to pieces. The only way to ward off the misfortune was to make pancakes, pancakes and more pancakes.

'You mustn't upset yourself, Bonnet. We are all ...' His boss had searched for the appropriate word – 'Mortal? Alike?' – but held back, from embarrassment, perhaps, or fear. 'OK. Have some rest and come back to us soon.'

Right, that was sorted, indefinite sick leave. It seemed just like any other day, however. Bernard felt no worse than the day before. Decidedly better in fact. The two days after Serge's First Communion had been a veritable agony: vomiting, migraines, an intense feeling of malaise. Then, on making this decision, a sort of respite. 'It's a question of attitude, Monsieur Bonnet,' Machon said. Perhaps he was right; they were mysterious, the body and the mind. Of those two days spent at the mercy of Yolande's whims and the vagaries of his physical condition, all he had left was 'room' in his life, 'room' like in a garment which is too big. Someone who knew about such things had once told him you shouldn't be able to see any light between two good dancers. His dancing days were over, and that was that, except with Yolande, of course, for the light had never been visible between them. As for his boss and his colleagues, he knew he wouldn't be seeing them again. It was no sadder than casting off an old pair of slippers. In taking leave, he had married death, and death fitted him like a glove. Sorrow came from denial – that was why life had so often made him suffer. Now he would say 'yes' to everything, good and bad, sunshine and grey skies alike; this November afternoon it was the latter.

Sitting behind the wheel of his car in the station car park, he felt desperately free. Doubtless this was how someone felt on the first day of unemployment: 'I could go here, or there, do nothing, go home and be bored stiff, go mad ...' The excess of freedom knocked him sideways. Maybe he should start collecting stamps, or keep pigeons like the retired men in these parts? Or build model ships? It was too much, too ...

An urgent rapping on the window made him jump. Roland's face, squashed up against the glass, looked strangely distorted, like a portrait by Bacon, streaming with rain.

'Bernard, help me! Féfé's just been run over by a lorry.'
'Who?'
'Féfé, my gun dog. Let me in.'
A smell of frying came off Roland as he got in beside Bernard. His eyes were glassy from tears and the rain.
'Shit, shit, shit!'
Bernard let him drum his fingers on the dashboard.
'He's one of a kind, that dog!'

'Calm down. What's going on?'

'My parents just phoned. I left Féfé with them for the weekend. I told them to keep him tied up! He always goes chasing after lorries!'

'Is he dead?'

'If only! I have to go and finish him off. I'm not brave enough. I saw you getting into your car and thought you …'

'I'd what?'

'Well … that you'd be able to … Don't make me do this on my own.'

Roland was leaking all over, from his eyes, nose and hair. He was the last of that ridiculous breed, the Sunday huntsmen who shoot at anything that moves, or not, as the case might be (he was the one to thank for the shot-riddled 'Caution. Children' sign on the way into the village), and now he was crying over his Féfé, half flattened by a lorry. A man who would swear on his deathbed that he loved animals. His own. He was a stupid, sad bastard, but at this moment Bernard could not bring himself to treat him as such. He knew he was a stupid bastard, a stupid bastard who hated him, but a stupid bastard who was weeping, the way the sky weeps, sometimes.

'Why me?'

'I couldn't bring myself to pull the trigger. Féfé and I … I just couldn't. But you know death.'

'Not yet, I don't.'

'You've seen it. I can tell you've seen it!'

'You're still drunk, Roland.'

'True, but it's because I'm suffering. You're the only one who can do it. Bernard, please …'

'Where d'your parents live?'

'Over by Brissy.'

Black and white like an old Chaplin film, minus the laughs. The sky could not decide whether to be bright or not. Most annoying. They parked outside Roland's parents' place, a once elegant house, which had been revamped with garden gnomes and fake wells made from tyres, like something out of a bad novel. Roland emerged, carrying a .22 rifle.

'Over there, by the bridge.'

Bernard parked. As they got out, Roland handed him the gun. They walked along the verge, the grass green against a backdrop of grey sky. It was a little slippery. In a dip in the bank, the tan and white dog, with a vacant look and his tongue lolling, was lying stretched out on his side. His back legs were now just a wet mush of hair and blood.

'Oh damn! Kill him, kill him!'

Bernard aimed the barrel at the back of the animal's ear, as it looked up at him, eyes growing dim. *Why me?*

It was a small rifle and the noise it made going off was no louder than a fart under the bedclothes. One click – and lights out. The dog's head fell back on to the soft grass. *A gully of green … foaming trough of light …*

Behind Bernard, Roland was busy throwing up.

'What do we do now?'

'Bin bag. In the car …'

Bernard took charge of everything. The dog was nothing but a piece of rubbish.

'What next?'

'How should I know? Better dig a hole.'

'Go on then.'

'Bloody hell, you're cruel!'

'I'm a killer not a gravedigger. There's a spade in the boot – off you go.'

Nowhere, here was nowhere. Unconsciously, while Roland was digging a hole for his dog, Bernard adopted the stance of the motorcyclist at the roadside. He smoked a cigarette; the sun was not there, however, and nor was the serenity which had made that moment special. At best, there was the complicity between two killers, one of them too cowardly to do the deed. The cigarette butt he flicked down on the wet tarmac was out in less than three seconds.

'I'm done. We can go.'

Roland was green, the colour of goose shit.

'That's another reason you'll have to be angry with me.'

'What?'

'I'm the person who killed your dog. Who will you have to complain about once I'm gone?'

'There's always someone. Do you think you're the only man who's screwed Jacqueline?'

Bernard smiled. If nothing else, humans were marvellously resourceful.

Getting out of the car outside the restaurant, Roland did not say thank you. He ran off, jacket up over his head, a hunched figure. People never said thank you to those who did their dirty work for them.

He already knew which dog he would buy next.

The same, no doubt. Roland always bought the same car, and if Jacqueline were to die he would find another one. A Nadine or a Martine maybe, but a Jacqueline even so. There are people like that, who think they can make things last for ever if they try hard enough.

For the past hour, Bernard had been driving around aimlessly, turning left here and right there, as luck or misfortune would have it. He had no idea where he was going but one thing he was sure about, he had no desire to go home, not straight away. Like a fly trapped under a glass he was looking for the way out while knowing only too well that none existed. As when he had left the station he felt burdened by the excess of freedom he was unable to use. Signposts pointed him in different directions: Lens, Liévin, Noeux-les-Mines, Béthune ... but they were traps, leading only to fields of mud crushed under the weight of the impending dark. Occasionally he passed through villages, brown brick houses set out like Lego belonging to a child devoid of imagination, blank windows hung with lace curtains depicting a pair of peacocks face to face or else plump cherubs in the same pose, and roofs topped with TV aerials resembling giant dragonflies. Who could possibly stop off in one of them, unless he had broken down? And yet people lived there, had their joys and sorrows no less than those who lived in picture postcard landscapes drenched in sunlight and azure. In those parts you would stop to buy regional pottery, local honey or to visit an old Romanesque church. Here there was nothing but home-brewed beer and war memorials of a soldier pointing his bayonet towards an indifferent sky, framed by four artillery shells with chains between them.

But you can't continue going nowhere for long, especially when night is falling, and so Bernard convinced himself he felt like eating moules-frites beside the station in Lille. It was years since he'd done that. He smiled at his own audacity. There was Yolande, it was true, but how could he let her know since she never answered the phone? In any case, she wasn't aware of the passage of time. And anyway, stuff Yolande, stuff Roland's dog, stuff it all! Illness made you self-centred, that was its greatest advantage.

He didn't order moules-frites but doughy, cheesy flammekueche. Inside Aux Brasseurs, once he had tucked himself away in a corner, he had felt so overwhelmed by all the noise, the belching and smoking throng – it was like something out of Breughel – that when the waiter had come to take his order he had asked for the same as the people at the next table, just to keep things simple. By now he was ruing his rashness. He hadn't even got a newspaper to read to make him look in command of the situation. This was taking ages, he'd already looked through the menu a dozen times. The clientele here were groups of friends or at least couples. Hang on, there was another man on his own. He even thought he recognised him as the travelling salesman who was cutting a swathe through the area, persuading lonely housewives to buy lingerie on credit, much to their husbands' anger. The man was eating mussels with no concern for the fact his loud slurping was getting on the other diners' nerves. He had the dispassionate and ice-cool air of a bounty hunter in a western. Or maybe it wasn't him after all. As a result of looking at people, since he had nothing else to do, Bernard ended up recognising everyone. That was odd, but not as improbable as all that. He had never left the area, and had seen a lot of people pass through the station. That said, no one recognised him. It was all an illusion, a whirl of faces seen here and there, a fug of beer and cigarette smoke. You rub shoulders with the whole world in a lifetime, but forget people again as you go along, like friends you make on holiday – you promise to keep in touch only to consign them to oblivion at once. How could it be otherwise? You'd need ten lifetimes to keep on top of all that. Besides, at the end of the day, we only need a few satellites to make up our galaxy. All stars are alike. That old pal Robert we were so fond of, who was lost in the mists of time, reappears one fine day calling himself Raoul or François or …

'Flammekueche with lardons!'

'For me, please.'

'Another beer?'

'Umm … all right.'

'Excuse me, Monsieur, but there's a lady on her own looking for a table, and there aren't any free. Would you mind if she shared yours?'

'Well, no, I …'

'Thank you, Monsieur. Madame? This way, please.'

She wasn't beautiful, she wasn't ugly, she almost wasn't, full stop, and yet she was very fat, first-rate camouflage.

'Good evening, Monsieur, thank you so much. It's so crowded here that it's hard to find a table if you're on your own.'

'Don't mention it, it's fine.'

'And this way, we're not on our own any more.'

They both gave an embarrassed little laugh, which lent them a family resemblance. Not wanting to appear as if she wished to invade Bernard's privacy, the lady pulled out a pair of glasses and a theatre programme which she began to study with a frown of concentration while she waited for her food. For Bernard the situation was even more embarrassing than when he had been alone. He tackled his flammekueche in small mouthfuls, dreading that at any moment he might drop slivers of onion or lardons on his lap. In any case, by halfway through his meal he was no longer hungry. He felt torn between the desire to run away as fast as his legs would carry him or to fall deeply asleep then and there. But he could do neither. The lady had already started on her grilled ham hock and he would have to ask her to stand up if he wanted to leave the table. He was doomed to spin out his beer for as long as he could, whilst affecting the air of someone wishing to enjoy the moment to the full. It was strange, but he felt he recognised her too. It wasn't her facial features, nor her general appearance but rather something in the way she chewed, switching her food from one cheek to the other with a twist of the lips. He was convinced of it now, he had eaten with this woman before. Sensing his gaze, heavy with beer, resting on her, the lady looked up. Bernard blushed, they smiled at each other awkwardly. This happened two or three times until nothing was left of the hock but a bone picked clean.

'We've met before, haven't we?'

'I don't know, but it seems like it. I didn't like to say. It

46

would have looked as if I was trying to take advantage of the situation.'

'I know what you mean. But no one would care, you know. If by any remote chance someone was interested in us, which I doubt, they would take us for a nice retired couple on their monthly night out.'

'Are you retired?'

'Yes, just recently. I'm getting used to it. Education. And yourself?'

'The same, but SNCF. Do you come from these parts?'

'I was born here and still have a few relatives in the area, but I live in Dijon.'

'Ah. But seriously, I do think I know you from somewhere.'

'That may be, one comes across so many people in a lifetime. Perhaps years ago, at school, or summer camp, at a dance ...'

'Possibly. No point in wondering about it. We wouldn't be the same now in any case.'

'That's true, but you can't help it, it's like a need to search for survivors around us. Other people's lives are annoying but they're also reassuring.'

'I apologise. I won't go on.'

'Don't worry. I feel the same.'

Really, it was better this way. As far as possible, Bernard avoided delving back into his youth. Not that his memories were any more painful than the next man's, it was just that his past seemed to him as cold and desolate as a deserted house.

At this point he might have left the table with a polite

'Lovely to make your acquaintance, good night, etc.'. He couldn't bring himself to do it, however. It was months since he had felt as much at ease as he did here. The lady seemed to find it agreeable as well, even though conversation had lapsed.

'Would you like another beer?'

'Yes, but somewhere else perhaps, it's so ... busy here ...'

'My name's Bernard.'

'And I'm Irène.'

They had just had two more beers in a red, velvety bistro, as snug as a fur muff. They had reached the stage of sharing experiences they had never had, those exquisite falsehoods exchanged by people whose paths have crossed and who will never see each other again.

Two insignificant lives transformed by the light filtering through the orange lampshades into unique and exotic existences, which still always brought them back in the end to: 'What now?'

Now all there was between them was two empty glasses and a skein of intertwined lives, the ends of which hung down pathetically on either side of the table. The sound system was on low, playing 'My Funny Valentine'. Chet Baker's voice comforted them in the great sorrow rising in their breast and bringing tears to their eyes.

'Not a bad choice for the closing credits.'

'Would you like me to see you back to your hotel?'

'No thanks, I'll get a taxi.'

'Why, when I've got my car outside?'

'OK, if you wish.'

The street was glistening after a slight drizzle. Irène slipped her arm through Bernard's.

'I think I'm a bit tiddly.'

Awkwardly, each one tried to adjust to the other's pace. Each step was a struggle, one step forwards and two steps back. The car was there waiting, though, as bright as a new pin. They got in. Irène's hand alighted on Bernard's as he went to start the ignition.

'Bernard, I would like you to kiss me.'

Their lips were cold, their tongues timid. There was a taste of the first time and dentures. Irène dissolved in tears on Bernard's shoulder.

'I'm sorry, it's been such a long time. I thought that was never going to happen to me again. Everything I've told you this evening is a lie. I've never travelled, I've never known great emotion, all my life I've been afraid of suffering so I've never experienced anything momentous. Nothing out of the ordinary has ever happened to me. Motorway, nothing but motorway, just grey monotony, with a few stops in lay-bys and breaks for frozen sandwiches. It'll soon be time to pay at the tollbooth and I'll have seen nothing, nothing at all. I don't want to go back to my hotel. Take me home with you, Bernard. Just for this one night – I'll leave in the morning, I promise!'

Yolande, Yolande, why must you always stand between me and the sun?

'Is that really what you want?'

'Yes. I've slept on my own almost all my life but tonight I really don't think I can face it.'

Irène was asleep by the time they reached the outskirts of Lille. Bernard was envious of her trust, how she let herself go, the unusual quality of her sleep. The dashboard lights cast a greenish glow around her profile. She slept the way children sleep, mouth slightly open, plump-lidded, unreachable.

Vimy, ten kilometres, diversion, roadworks ... Bernard set off into the depths of the night on an earth track, exuding inky dark. For several hundred metres now the headlights had picked up nothing at all. It was like the end of the earth.

The end of the earth was a building site. People had decided that it wasn't distant enough, and so they were extending it by spreading concrete over the nothingness. Bernard stopped and switched off the headlights. The absolute blackness gathered in his eyes until, little by little, he began to make out the gigantic shapes of the machines, silent gaping mouths ready to gobble up the sky once they had swallowed the earth.

He brushed Irène's soft cheek with his fingers and whispered, 'We're here.' Without waking, she moved her shoulder slightly as if to nudge a sheet back into place. Bernard could have sworn she was offering him her throat. Between his thumb and first finger, the Adam's apple went in and out, in and out, in and out ...

There wasn't much life left in the body. For a split second he saw Irène's pupil flicker then grow cloudy like that of Roland's dog. The life of one person had just passed into the body of the other. Bernard couldn't loosen his grip. He made the orgasm last until the pain went all the way up his arm to his shoulder, then to the very highest point of his crown, until it blew the top of his head off.

Then he got out of the car and fell on his knees in the mud.

'It's not my fault! I'm the only one who's dying!'

There was no echo in this place. The silence absorbed everything, like the sky, the earth, the concrete. Death mopped up life so that no trace of existence should sully the relentless onward march of the A26 autoroute.

Irène was not to have the same grave as Maryse. Despite scouring the whole of the building site, the best place Bernard could find was the cesspool covered by a small yellow corrugated-iron hut, which the workmen used as their dustbin and lavatories. Just at the moment the body sank into the cesspit, releasing appalling vapours, he remembered: Irène Lefébure. They used to have lunch sitting opposite each other in the school canteen. She wasn't an unpleasant girl but she'd repelled him a bit because of her bulimia, which meant that she used to finish everyone's leftovers. They'd called her 'the dustbin'.

As he was about to get back into the car, Bernard felt as if someone's gaze was burning into the back of his neck. The moon pierced the clouds like a cigarette hole in a blackout curtain. As with Maryse, the moon was full. Pure chance. But that wouldn't stop them talking of a serial killer, the full-moon murderer.

'WOMAN'S BODY FOUND ON SITE OF A26 WORKS
Workmen on the site made the grisly discovery late on Tuesday afternoon. The police have carried out initial investigations, which are proving very difficult. There has been so much digging and compacting of the ground by machinery that the state of the corpse makes identification impossible for the moment. It will be necessary to wait for the results of the ...'

Yolande was reading the newspaper, tracing the words with one finger and using another to swing her 'More than yesterday and much less than tomorrow' pendant from side to side like a pendulum. She was speaking in a singsong voice, like a child reciting a fable. Bernard kept his eyes fixed on the pendant.

'...the time to complete additional investigations ...

I know, why don't I bake an angel-hair cake tonight? You know, with lots of sugar. It's ages since I did that.'

'I'm not really very hungry.'

'It doesn't matter, I feel like making a cake. It's a day for it, and besides there are a lot of ends of packets.'

'If you like. Pass me some water, please. Thanks. Help me to drink, I can't lift my head.'

Bernard was searching for the rim of the glass. His eyesight was deteriorating. A whirl of rings with wavy outlines and dark insides was dancing in front of his eyes. The two mouthfuls of water came back up, and dribbled down his chin through his beard.

'You pig!'

Yolande went back to her reading.

'With the information currently available to the police and magistrates ...'

(What's she going to do with my dead body? Stuff it into the bottom of the wardrobe? Bodies everywhere, in the mud of the building site, at the back of cupboards...)

'It would be rash to link it to the disappearance of the young woman Maryse L ...

What's the point of me reading to you, Bernard, if you're not going to listen? Your mind's elsewhere. If you go on pretending to be dead like this, you really will die, so there. You're horrible to me, I'm going.'

Yolande was angry. He'd become a right pain with his illness, no time for anyone but himself. He'd been like that when he was little, snivelling at the slightest knock. Yolande had never been ill, ever. Let him hurry up and die, and that would be an end to it. She didn't know what it was he wanted. He could always hang himself if it was taking too long. People were always like that, complaining about their lives, going 'it's too hot' or 'it's too cold', 'I'm too young', 'I'm too old', etc. They only needed to follow her example and not like anything, that way you were never disappointed and other people got a bit of peace as well. She had nothing against her brother, mind you. All their lives the two of them had been like one and the same person, but whether you lost a tooth, a brother or an arm, there was no need to go overboard about it! In any case, it was for his benefit that she was making the angel-hair cake. It was a favourite recipe from *La Semaine de Suzette*. It was tasty, easy to make and filled you up nicely.

She trotted off into the kitchen, and poured all the ends of vermicelli packets into a salad bowl. There was an amazing amount. Pulling a saucepan out from under a heap of dirty dishes, she set off an avalanche of metalware.

'Oh shit! Filthy rotten bastards! Damn bitch of a saucepan!!!'

She kicked the floor clear. Of course, he was wallowing in bed all day, savouring each remaining drop of life, so obviously she was left to see to everything. Shaking with fury, she gave the saucepan, still coated with the remains of last night's noodles, a quick rinse under the tap.

'What've you done with the sugar? Oi, you!'

And yet the day had begun on a positive note, she'd been in a good mood when she'd got up. A shaft of light coming through a chink in the shutters had bounced off the white enamel of her bowl. That was all it had taken to bring back a whole flood of happy memories. Life was the way it was, but sometimes it gave gifts, even to people who didn't deserve them, even to wrong 'uns like her. That was in the way of things. After all, life killed off plenty of fine people, through wars, road accidents or illness. It was only right that it should make up for its stupid tricks.

The day they had drowned that bitch Fernande's cat, a lovely day. The old bag was always spreading evil gossip about her, hands clutching her windowsill, with her mangy cat wedged between her huge tits.

'That Yolande's been seen leaving the dance with ...'

Yolande wouldn't have minded going with all the local boys she talked about. There hadn't been as many as all that, but it still got her a tanning with the razor strop as soon as her father heard about it. Titi, that cat's name was. It stank. By promising Bernard a lollipop, she had talked him into distracting the old girl long enough for her to stuff the tomcat into a potato sack. Then they'd run to the bomb crater, the one where you could fish for frogs, and she had weighted the sack with pebbles. Inside the cloth, Titi had made a token effort at wriggling. Perhaps he thought it was a game – you could never tell, where children were concerned.

Yolande had whirled the sack round above her head

before flinging it right into the middle of the pool with a loud 'ha!' The water had broken into a rippling smile before it grew perfectly impassive again, like a pool of oblivion. Bernard had clung to his sister's skirt.

'That's a crime, isn't it, Yoyo? You've committed a crime.'

'Of course not, it's only a cat. Serves it right, ugly beast.'

Yolande had lain full length on the bank, hands behind her head, serene, in the satisfaction of a job well done. Her skirt was hitched up to her thighs, letting in the soft April breeze. A flock of white clouds grazed on the blue overhead. Soon it would be Easter. She was seventeen and longing to get stuck in to all that the world had to offer. On the wireless the talk was of nothing but war, today, tomorrow, or the day after, and of Chancellor Hitler who was frightening everyone except her. If he was really such a bogeyman, that chap, then all the big noises spouting into the microphones had only to do what she'd done, stick him in a sack and throw it into a bomb crater. But oh no, they preferred to scare one another, holding up the spectre of war at arm's length like a scarecrow forming a perch for crows. War, in weather like this, it was a joke! Here, war, 1870, 1914, and earlier still, was just a part of life. All it had left behind were holes you could drown feline collaborators in and where kids fished for frogs. No need to get so worked up about it! In any case, people didn't go to war when the weather was so fine. All these people needed was a good lay and they'd forget about fighting. Backside, pussy, prick, eating, sleeping, like in primitive paintings or on the walls of the toilets in the station or cafés, nothing but pleasure, then, at the end, a sack weighted with stones and a hole in the water. That was what life meant for her, and that should be enough for the whole of humanity.

The foolish young sun drying its rays above the pale-green shoots carpeting the fields seemed to agree with her. The less you thought, the more you lived, and whatever you could take was one fewer thing for the Boches to get. The Boches or someone else, stupidity didn't stop at borders. She was at this point in her reflections when Bernard had started yelling: 'Yoyo! Help, Yoyo, I'm drowning!' The sack with Titi in it was lying by the edge of the water near a long wooden rod, and in the middle of the pond her brother was flailing about as he went under. Yolande had leapt into the thick black liquid. It wasn't very deep, maybe two metres in the centre, but the little idiot had got his foot caught in some scrap metal and couldn't get it free again. She had had trouble extricating him, he was panicking and yelling at the top of his voice. Finally she'd succeeded in pulling him to the bank by his hair. They had flopped down, panting, beside the sack swollen with water, stones and Titi, now defunct. They stank of mud. Black bubbles were still bursting on the surface of the crater, letting off smells of infernal farts.

'Are you mad or something? It's full of God knows what in there. Why d'you do that?'

'I just slipped, Yoyo. I didn't want Titi to die. I thought a good ducking would be enough.'

'Well, he's dead anyway, and you could have ended up the same way, you little shit. Let's see your ankle.'

It was all swollen, bloody like raw steak. Yolande had torn a strip from her dress to use as a bandage.

'Yoyo?'

'What?'

'You stink.'

'So do you.'

They'd rolled around on the grass, laughing like things possessed. Coated in mud all over, they'd slithered into each other's arms like eels. Yolande had poked her tongue into his mouth to make him be quiet. Her brother's body had juddered between her thighs and then for one brief moment everything was still. War itself could not have divided them. The silence had something of eternity about it. Then a frog jumped into the water. Yolande sat up again, the blue of her eyes had darkened to violet. Bernard was smiling, eyes closed like a child asleep, lips slightly parted. Yolande had remembered a poem she'd read at school, about a young soldier lying dead in a verdant spot bathed in sunlight. It had ended with 'Nature, cradle him gently, he is cold' or some such.

'You'll never do that.'

'What?'

'Fight their stupid war. You'll be like me, you'll live for ever.'

With one kick, she'd consigned Titi to his ineluctable fate once more and they'd gone home. For that one day, Yolande had been treated like a queen, she had saved her little brother's life. No one had picked quarrels with her. The best thing of all had been hearing fat Fernande calling for her cat.

Now Bernard had spoilt everything. His illness had made him selfish, he had no time for her any more. At a corner of the table, Yolande was mixing vermicelli and caster sugar.

Even seen full on, Bernard was now only a profile, with a lipless black hole in place of a mouth. What life he had left was lurking there, in that well of shadows, evident only in shallow gusts of foul-smelling breath. He no longer knew whether he was awake or asleep, there was no difference, just the same state on repeat for almost a week now. Fragments of the newspaper article would come back to him: 'Grisly discovery, police, woman's body …' Each word was so charged with meaning that a whole sentence would throw him into complete and utter confusion. He wasn't afraid for himself, the A26 was swarming with foreign workers – Spaniards, Turks, North Africans – almost 250 firms were at work on the section, 700 workers, that was where the finger of suspicion pointed. And in any case, what could they do to him? Life had already condemned him for a crime he had not committed, being born without intent. There were a lot of words ending in 'ion' in the article: 'investigations, identification, conclusions, etc'. After that he amused himself by making a string of other words ending in 'ion': circulation, ascension, passion, circumvolution. That one was a beauty, a graceful swirl. Recitation: '*La cigale ayant chanté tout l'été se trouva fort dépourvue quand la bise fut venue.*' Mademoiselle Leny, his primary school teacher, used to pronounce it 'la Biiiise!' Her eyebrows would shoot right up to the top of her forehead when she said 'la Biiise!'

Yolande had been the one to teach him how to kiss, and to masturbate, but that was later. They'd almost gone the whole way once. One Thursday afternoon, when he'd had flu. It was winter, in the last year of the war. She was cold and had lain down next to him in the bed. People were cold the whole time, coal was hard to find. He was worried that she would catch his germs, but she'd said she didn't care, she was stronger than they were. They'd been looking at a film magazine. She was deliberately lingering over the pages showing scantily dressed film stars: 'What about her, doesn't that make you feel anything when you look at her? Her legs, there ...' In a flash, one fever had been replaced by another. There were no flies on his pyjamas, the cord at his waist was cutting into him. It was Yolande who had undone it. Slowly, Bernard's hand had made its way up under his sister's skirt. He'd stopped at the first hairs, at the top of her thighs, not daring to venture further, into the unknown jungle. The elastic material of her knickers was stretched tight, a yielding shell which fitted neatly into the palm of his hand. He had lain on top of her, burning up, drenched in sweat. Yolande had opened her legs and pulled her pants out of the way, while her other hand guided Bernard into position. But at the moment of penetration, she had pushed him sharply away.

As for the rest, he no longer remembered. He must have masturbated, in all probability.

'I'm dying, and I've got a hard-on.'

Nothing else had ever happened between him and his sister.

'I find him more disgusting every day. He's drunk by ten in the morning, and every evening I get a pasting because some customer has been giving me the eye, or for any old thing. Shall I tell you what? I wish he'd die.'

'That'll happen.'

'Yes, but when?'

Jacqueline was making huge figures of eight with her cloth on the waxed tablecloth. There wasn't so much as a crumb of Bernard's lunch left, but she carried on, as if she were trying to rub off the brown and yellow floral pattern on the tablecloth or something even more stubborn, Roland's life for instance. She had her sleeves rolled up to the elbow. Bernard had always loved her arms, strong, hands reddened from washing up. It must be good to sleep in arms like those.

'You're not listening to me – where are you?'

'Yes, I am, I'm here.'

'No, you're here but you're not here. You look like a

saint in a church, smiling at everything but not seeing a thing.'

'I don't know. It's as if I've been away somewhere. I recognise things and people, but it's all changed ever so slightly, like the tracing on top of a drawing that's moved by a fraction of a millimetre. I don't know how to explain it to you.'

'I've not heard from you for a whole week. Were you having a rough time?'

'That's putting it mildly. But yes, I really thought I'd had it. Death comes closer, like the sea, it hits me full in the face, a huge wave of black foam. I tell myself the time has come, in my head I've packed my bag, and then it draws away again. It'll be back.'

'Aren't you scared?'

'Not any more. When I was a kid on holiday at the beach, I used to practise walking with my eyes closed, in case I went blind some day. It's the same sort of thing.'

'You're going and then you come back – is that what you're saying?'

'If you like.'

'If it was me, I wouldn't come back.'

'You don't get to decide, you just have to go along with it.'

'What about the pain?'

'That's what keeps us alive. Without the pain or even just the fear of pain we'd all be off at the first unhappy love affair.'

'That might not be such a bad thing.'

'I don't know about that. All I know is, if you're still here, it must be for a good reason.'

'Oh well, do enlighten me then, because I can't for the life of me think what it is!'

'Yet you are here.'

'Barely ... Why, Bernard, why have we spent our whole time walking alongside our own lives?'

Jacqueline's lower lip was beginning to stick out and tremble, her eyes misted over. Her face was so close to Bernard's that he could see nothing else, as if all there was in the world was this woman's face, ravaged by regret and steeped in exhaustion. It was as though he were looking at her through a magnifying glass – wrinkles, hairs, blackheads – it was hardly proper. It was life that had caused all this damage, like a river gouging out its course down a mountain, day after day, for so many days. And behind those eyes damp with tears was a little girl struggling, trying to get out of there, beating her fists against the glass walls of the jar in which she'd been suffocating for ...

'I don't know where you've gone, Bernard, but you've no right to leave me here, no right at all. One day I'm going to do something stupid, I'll get a gun and blow that bastard Roland's head off and I'll do the same to your bitch of a sister ...'

'Be quiet, Jacqueline. You're talking nonsense now. Some things can't be killed with a gun because they're dead already.'

'You're talking like a dead man. But I'm still alive. Go away, you're even worse than the rest, nothing can affect you any more.'

Jacqueline got up so abruptly that her chair toppled over backwards. She righted it again so violently it was as if she wanted to drive it into the floor. The bang echoed awhile in the empty room of the restaurant. Bernard's hand still smelt of Jacqueline's: disinfectant and floorcloth. An hour before, there had been lots of people here, eating macaroni and roast pork amid noisy laughter. No trace of them now, as if they'd been imaginary. Life was about being there when things happened, if not it was a desert. People appeared and disappeared and you never knew where they'd come from or where they were headed. Paths simply crossed.

When Bernard tried to pay for his meal, Jacqueline told him to go to hell, without even turning round.

The rat caught the full force of Yolande's slipper.

'A rat's at home anywhere. Comes from goodness knows where and never gets where it's going. The thing goes from one house to another, making tunnels for itself all over the place. No limits at all. Dirty beast! That bastard of a butcher came by just now. He sounded his horn several times. Usually Bernard puts his order in on a Tuesday. But he's not here, he's never here, even when he is here. Oh well, we won't be eating meat any more, it's as simple as that. Or else we'll have rat. If he's not in his bed pretending to be dead for days on end he's disappearing off somewhere. "I've got to keep myself busy," that's what he says. As if! He's joined the Resistance and doesn't want to tell me. The Boches have taken over his body but he's holding out against them with his mind. I've seen right through him. He must be derailing trains, that's his thing, trains. I see him come home with his conspirator's face on. As if you couldn't tell he's killing Boches! Once a fellow's killed another fellow, he's not the same any more. I remember Zep, Zep's short for Joseph, Joseph Haendel, that was the name of my Boche. One day he was in a platoon which had to kill some hostages. When I saw him the next day he wasn't the same man. You'd have thought he'd lost something precious, like an arm or a leg. He was looking all around, he seemed distracted. At night he would wake up yelling things in German that I couldn't understand: "*Nein! Nein! ...*" drenched in sweat. He was a good country lad, Zep, a Bavarian. Pigs, hens, ducks, rabbits, he'd slit their throats by the dozen, but the hostages, that he just couldn't stomach. You can't eat people, I wonder if that was why. Always looking over his shoulder. And before him, all he could see was the Russian front. A rat in a trap, that's what my fine Zep had become. All the men became Ripolin Brothers, lined up one behind the other like in the paint adverts, but it wasn't paintbrushes they were holding, it was daggers. Row upon row, their white tunics stained with blood like that bastard of a butcher. "I kill you, you kill me." And the more they killed, the more of them sprang up again, it was truly miraculous! That's why there'll never be an end to the war – anyway, it's always been here, it's that kind of country, there's nothing else to do but go to war. The only thing that grows is white crosses. Even Bernard's not been able to keep out of it. But what the hell, let them go on tearing each other to bits. It makes sod all difference to me!'

Yolande went back to the needlework which had been interrupted by the incident with the rat. She was sewing scraps together, pieces of silk and ends of lace, on to what was left of a red dress, and humming '*Couchés dans le foin*'. She got up and stood before the wardrobe mirror, holding the extraordinary garment up in front of her, stepped back a little, primped and posed, tried out a few dance steps and burst out laughing.

'I don't give a damn about the Resistance! You're all made like rats! You've all lost!'

Whenever Bernard went out prowling around aimlessly, sooner or later he would find himself beside the railway. Sometimes he stood on the bridge above the tunnel and waited for the trains to go by. He knew them all, the 16.18, the 17.15 … He would see them coming in the distance then being swallowed up, almost as if inside him, with a din of metal on metal that shook the handrail he was leaning on. Shutting his eyes, he would count how many seconds they took to pass right through. He had already seen himself toppling and trains running over him. He'd imagined the scene a dozen times, the engine hurtling on at top speed and cutting him in two like an earthworm. Always at the end of this dream, however, his two halves would be wriggling on either side of the track and would manage to stick themselves together again. Bernard would find himself in one piece, walking along the rails with no idea where he was going. Rails leading to more rails … Today he was hanging around the warehouses of the disused goods station. Beneath the tall metal structure there was a raised platform where the wagons used to be loaded, with straw, or livestock, up to fifteen times a day sometimes. Dozens of men had worked here. Where were they now? The police kept an eye on the place. People said youngsters came here to get up to mischief, smash the few remaining windows, take drugs. So they said. The concrete paving slabs had burst under the pressure of irrepressible vegetation. Tons of steel and cement would never be a match for the puniest blade of grass. All that work for nothing. What if Bernard were the only survivor of some cosmic disaster? And if there were no one left in the world but him, rattling around all on his own in this deserted shed? Then, if death laid eggs in his stomach, what if he was the first man on earth and everything was going to begin all over again with him? On the walls was obscene graffiti, of erect penises, and legs spread wide, which reminded him of points on the tracks. They'd been boldly drawn in chalk, or scratched using a sharpened stone. This was Lascaux, this was the dawn of humanity, hunting scenes. Men had lived here. Even after countless centuries they still had nothing to express but the need to procreate, to have sex, over and over again. What price evolution?

'Hey, Granddad, what do you think you're doing?'

A young guy with eyes like a cat was staring at him, sniggering, sitting on a beam with his legs dangling in mid-air, two metres up.

'Nothing, just taking a walk. I used to work here a long time ago.'

'Long ago, so you're a dinosaur then?'

'I was just thinking that myself.'

'Have you got a fag?'

'No, I don't smoke.'

It was like a circus act. The young man threw himself backwards, bounced off the wall, catapulted off a heap of old planks and landed at Bernard's feet.

'You could have been killed!'

'Don't worry on my account, old man. Don't you know it's dodgy around here?'

'So they say.'

'Aren't you afraid?'

'What would I be afraid of?'

'Me.'

'Sorry, but to be honest, no, I'm not frightened of you.'

'Funny, you don't look all that tough.'

'I don't understand – what is it you're after?'

The young man sprang to one side, flicking open a knife.

'Your wallet, you old prick, or I'll fucking kill you!'

'Oh, is that all? Here you are.'

Bernard smiled and reached for his coat pocket. The young man, thrown by Bernard's attitude, moved back.

'Wait! You're weird. What are you so happy about? What've you got in your pocket, a gun?'

'Of course not, I swear.'

'Don't move!'

'I must have two or three hundred francs, take it.'

'Don't move I said!'

Bernard took a step forward and put his hand in his coat pocket. The youth shrank back in panic, his foot met with empty air, and he toppled backwards. Bernard didn't have time to catch him. He disappeared over the edge of a platform, making a strange sound like someone taking a deep breath before diving underwater. Bernard rushed forwards. There he was, a kid twisting and turning on the rusty rails, dry grass growing between them, with his own knife sticking out of his chest.

'Don't hurt me, M'sieur! Call an ambulance!'

'Of course I won't. It's an accident, don't be scared ...'

The kid's hand clutched at his sleeve. His gaze turned blue, like a newborn baby's. A bubble of blood burst at the corners of his mouth.

'Don't do this to me, kiddo!'

One last spasm and the young man was no more than a piece of rubbish, a disused shell like the shed open to the elements on all sides. On his knees beside the corpse, Bernard lifted his eyes to the rusty iron sky. He no longer dared lay a finger on anything, for fear of seeing humans, things or animals crumble to dust at his touch. He had become the instrument of death, death itself. He felt no guilt, death being a psychosomatic illness, but he was astonished by its lightning speed.

Fifteen minutes earlier, the kid hadn't existed, any more than Bernard had existed for him. Then wham! – the young man had come to life for just a matter of minutes, the lifespan of a clay pipe at a shooting gallery. As for him, in some strange way his imminent and inescapable death seemed to make him immortal. Rising in his chest was not a sob but a burst of laughter, straight from the heart, of the kind that seizes you when words fail. Bernard wondered how he was going to drag the body – by the feet? Under the arms? They say there is nothing heavier than an empty heart; the same is true of a lifeless body. It is life that holds us upright, which gives us that lightness of being. Without life the bones, the flesh weigh tons. But why go to all that trouble? He had nothing to do with it this time. What was the point of wearing himself out to plant this seed of death beneath the A26? Force of habit. He could, he supposed, go to the police station and explain what had happened. The idea made him smile. But he was too tired to play that game. The young man would do very well where he was, lying with his cheek against these rails which led nowhere. It was the most fitting end for someone who had gone down the wrong track. Bernard turned his coat collar up. It was cold. In the sky the dark was spreading like a pool of ink. A sprinkling of stars appeared. Bernard aimed his finger and rubbed out a few. Every second, some of them died, people said. What did that matter when four times as many were born in the same time? The sky was an enormous rubbish tip.

Bernard walked off, sniffing. He could feel he was getting a cold. Once in the car, before starting the engine, he looked for a tissue in the glove compartment. There was one left, a used one. While he was wiping his nose, the beam of headlights came sweeping over the countryside and slowed as it drew level with him. Bernard turned his back. That was what was so annoying about nature – whenever you thought you were on your own some country bumpkin popped up from behind a hedge. But the car picked up speed again and disappeared, leaving a scarlet glow-worm trailing behind.

Yolande's soup consisted of some leftover cabbage, a tin of ravioli in tomato sauce, two potatoes, a chicken carcass, a handful of lentils, a vanilla pod and two or three other ingredients she couldn't quite recall. While emptying the cupboards into the large cooking pot she had said to herself that her recipe would be called 'Everything must go'.

'Is it nice?'

'It's unusual – what is it?'

'Slum-it soup. You weren't here when the butcher came. You're having what there is.'

'I'm sorry. I'll go shopping tomorrow.'

'Have you been out derailing a train again?'

'What are you talking about?'

'Do you think I'm an idiot? I know your little game, it's an open secret. To be honest, I couldn't care less, if it makes you happy. But damn, I could have murdered an escalope!'

'I'll get some tomorrow, I promise. It's not bad, this soup. A little … exotic maybe.'

Obediently, Bernard cleaned his plate. Yolande left hers untouched, giving him her china-doll stare.

'So you'll eat any old thing and say nothing to me?'

'I said I liked it, Yoyo.'

'That's not what I'm talking about! My dress?'

'Oh yes. It's beautiful. It could almost be the one you were wearing the day …'

'Aha, so you do … I found it in the wardrobe. I've added a few frills and some lace round the collar.'

'Of course! It's very pretty. Stand up, turn round … Splendid!'

A slight blush crept over Yolande's cheeks. She went back and forth, twirled around the table. Bernard turned the pendant lamp on her as a spotlight.

'If our thick bastard of a father had just let me move to Paris I'd have been another Chanel. And there's nothing to it, you know, just reusing some old bits and bobs. It can't have taken me more than a couple of hours!'

'It's a masterpiece. Really.'

'And it goes nicely with that little chain you gave me: "Less than yesterday and three times as much as tomorrow".'

'More than yesterday and much less than tomorrow.'

'Same difference. I'll have to make myself a coat to go with it. Could you give me your old SNCF one? You won't need it any more, you're going to die.'

'Of course. Yolande, shall we dance?'

'All right. I adore you.'

They couldn't really have said what they were

73

celebrating, Yolande's amazing dress, the death of the young man, the unspeakable mush congealing on their plates or simply a moment of grace which had strayed into this place which had known so few, but they did it with all their heart. Bernard waltzed his sister around; she was laughing, head flung back and white hair flying like an ashen cloud. Round and round they whirled, heedless of the furniture they bumped into as they went past, knocking things over, raising flurries of dust and scaring a rat off its dustbin feast. The world could have stopped turning and they would still have continued their drunken waltz atop its ruins, to the accompaniment of Yolande's reedy tones as she sang softly: '*J'attendrai, le jour et la nuit, j'attendrai toujours, ton retour …*' The swaying ceiling light was a makeshift glitter ball, multiplying their shadows on the walls. They were a whole ballroom, just the two of them. What else, who else could they ever need? Bernard surrendered to the ever faster rhythm forced on him by his sister. Eternity must be like this whirl, a gigantic food mixer, blending bodies into one paste, one wave crashing into oblivion. Bernard lost his footing, stumbled and fell full length on the floor.

'You wretch! Give up now, would you?'

Yolande took hold of him by the collar and tried to get him on his feet again. Bernard opened his mouth but couldn't make even the slightest sound. His body no longer responded to the orders issued by his brain. He was in unknown territory.

'Shift your backside, will you! Hang on, have some wine, that'll sort you out.'

He saw his sister stride over him, her legs as spindly as a chair's. He heard her uncorking a bottle. She came back and poured the wine straight from the bottle into his mouth. Bernard couldn't swallow any longer. He could understand everything, see everything, hear everything but he no longer knew what to do to live. He didn't have the instructions any more. Apart from this feeling of panic he wasn't suffering, unless he'd forgotten how to do that as well.

'Dance! You mustn't stop dancing, not ever!'

Dragging him like a broken puppet, Yolande hoisted him on to her back and walked him round the room. Bernard's gaze fixed on the corner of the table, a patch of wall, a myriad of tiny details it seemed he was seeing for the first time, pencil marks on the doorframe with the legend 'Bernard aged six, Yolande aged eight', all the things a bull must see when the horses are dragging it out of the ring. Nothing hurt, there was just the strange feeling that he'd forgotten something, like when you leave the house and wonder whether you've turned the gas off properly.

Exhausted, Yolande walked him round the table one last time before putting him down on his bed. She collapsed on to a bedside chair.

'See where your stupid tricks have got you? Everyone who plays at war ends up like you. But you won't listen to me, you will go out playing the hero. I'm going to make you a nice eggnog. There's nothing like eggnog.'

The last thing Bernard saw was a monstrous hen pecking away with the tip of its beak at an endless worm.

'A settling of scores, I don't think so!'

'And why not? There's a whole load of junkies hanging around the depot. The guy the police found was one of them. His arms were covered in needle marks, from what they're saying.'

'And the remains of the woman they found in the works on the A26, was she an addict? And the kid who's never been found, she was one too, was she?'

'There's no connection, Roland.'

'Hmm, well, I think there is, and I've got my own theory about it, what's more.'

'Out with it then!'

'I know what I mean. And when the time comes, there'll be quite a few who won't know what's hit them. Whose round is it?'

There were just three of them left propping up the bar, noses in their beer. Roland was at the pump. He couldn't wait for them to clear off. At this time of day he was as prickly as a hedgehog, everything got to him. All he wanted to do was sit down in front of the TV and stuff himself with sounds and pictures to the point of oblivion. The dog he'd bought to replace Féfé was a non-starter, he'd had to take it back to the kennels that afternoon. He'd given them a piece of his mind and no mistake. The Strasbourg–Monaco match scheduled for that evening had been postponed because of bad weather. And all these dickheads could talk about was the young man who'd been found stabbed in the disused warehouse of the old goods station. No need to get upset over him. One little shit more or less — who was counting? But on his way back from his parents' in Brissy, it was definitely Bernard's Renault 5 that he'd seen parked near the shed. Naturally he hadn't said a word to anyone. His little secret, he was hugging it close, so he could come out with it at the right moment. For years now he'd had him in his sights, that Bernard. Right family of lunatics, him and his tart of a sister. Never mind that they were local, one of these days it was all going to go up, and it would be him, Roland, who set it off. And that slut Jacqueline would have to shut her big mouth. He'd always known he was a pervert, that bloke, with his 'butter wouldn't melt' act. Even as a small child he'd been like that, doing things on the sly and hiding in his sister's skirts as soon as things went badly for him. All the things that had happened in the neighbourhood, the kid who'd vanished, the body on the building site and that little toerag the other evening, it had all started the day Bernard left his job at the station. Always prowling around in his Renault 5, or disappearing off. If someone went to the bother of digging around in that direction they'd turn up some interesting things, that was for sure! You'd only had to see him put a bullet in poor Féfé's head, hadn't so much as batted an eyelid, not a moment's hesitation, bang!

'OK, Roland, we're off now. See you tomorrow.'

'Right, see you tomorrow.'

Roland bolted the door behind them. He was about to leave the room when he met his own gaze looking back at him, that of a tall blond young man, a good head taller than the rest of the football team in a yellowing photo which had pride of place between two trophies and three pennants. Nothing got past him into the net in those days, people respected him. He could have turned professional if he'd wanted. Why hadn't he wanted? Not finding an answer to that question, he told himself it was because of Jacqueline. She had to be of use for something. Couldn't even give him kids – or do the dusting. Roland whisked the cloth from his shoulder and gave the two cups a polish. Then he turned out the lights and climbed wearily up the stairs to the flat.

There were dozens of buttons, hundreds even, scattered over the table. Tiny ones in mother-of-pearl, little half-spheres with painted flowers on them, leather buttons, wooden buttons, some in horn and others covered with fabric. Yolande's fingers caressed them, sorted through them, mixed them up, married and divorced them and began all over again, untiringly. She had boxes full. Before emptying out a new one she would plunge her hands into it, like a miser with his gold. Bernard had passed away at around one in the morning.

She had not been at his bedside. A kind of gap had opened in the silence while she was making vigorous cuts in the SNCF overcoat. She had gone into his room. He had the same over-earnest look as in his school photographs. A complete act, anything for a quiet life. It hadn't mattered what anyone thought of him just as long as they left him in peace. His watch had stopped at eleven forty-five. He must have said to himself that his train was late. He'd been looking at his watch constantly in recent days. She'd wondered momentarily where she was going to put him, before telling herself he was in as good a place as any. As for the escalopes, that was scuppered, he wouldn't be buying any more now.

The Big blue coat button family ran into the Mother-of-pearl shirt button family. 'How are you today? Shall we go for a walk? Tip-tap-tip.'

Four days of Siberian chill. Nothing was moving on the plain, the cold took even the wind's breath away. Work on the A26 site had been brought to a standstill. The silence was such that you could hear a frozen branch snap like a glass straw from a mile away. It no longer seemed like death even, more like the time before life, before life had even been thought of. Yolande spent hours face to face with the cooker, as rigid as the chair she was sitting on, chewing the inside of her cheeks. Four days, four years, four hundred years … And then the chap had rung the doorbell. When no one answered, he'd knocked several times. He took a few steps back and looked upwards. All the shutters were closed. He scribbled a quick note on his knee and slipped it under the door. Yolande was watching him through the world's arsehole. She'd waited for him to disappear off in his little blue car before seizing on the note. 'Hello Bernard! Down at the station we're wondering how you are. Give us a ring or join us for a drink. See you soon, Simon.'

Yolande folded the note in two, then in four, in six, then eight, till it was no bigger than a pill and she swallowed it.

Others would come. She would swallow them all. She'd swallow everything. That's what she'd do. Everything could be eaten. The rats were eating Bernard, Yolande would eat the rats. With garden peas. She had loads of them. Bernard didn't like them but he'd always got a tin when he did the week's shopping. It was a tradition. There were sardines as well, plenty of them, and tomato sauce. She had all she needed, several times over. She had the wherewithal to live two lives here, two lives sheltered from others. She could do it all herself. She needed no one else. Music, for example, on that mandolin. She knew a tune: 'Ramona ... I'll always remember the rambling rose you wore in your hair.'

'Bugger off!'

The mandolin narrowly missed the rat running across the table. The echo of the instrument made ripples on the surface of the silence. Yolande closed her eyes. The same movement in the darkness inside her head.

'Don't lean out of the window, Yoyo, you'll get your head torn off if we go through a tunnel.' It would all be going so fast that it was impossible to open your eyes or even breathe. Now and then you'd get tiny smuts in your face. The tears in the corner of your eyes would be drawn upwards and vanish into your hair, streaming backwards with the wind. It took a smack across the legs to make her come away from the window and sit quietly on the seat. The intoxication would last for quarter of an hour and then she'd be at it again, on the pretext that she felt travel sick. That's how she would have liked to go through life, eyes closed, at the window of a train hurtling onwards, at the risk of getting her head torn off in a tunnel. They'd made do with shaving it.

Yolande had thought Bernard had moved, but no, it was a rat, a big fat rat under the bedcover. She hadn't missed that one, eliminating it with one blow from the dictionary, open at the page with the D's: deride, derision, derisory, etc. Afterwards she'd dissected the animal with her little sewing scissors, ever so neatly. She'd cooked it in red wine like a rabbit, a rabbit the right size for her, a one-portion rabbit.

She was alone in the world now, surrounded by miniature rabbits, rather like Alice in Wonderland. After dinner she would play the little horse game, while she dipped biscuits into a thimbleful of red wine. She would be both Bernard and Yolande. When she was Yolande she would cheat, of course.

The dice was stuck on five. Besides the unseen presence of mice and rats, nothing moved. The pendant lamp still cast its forty watts of greyish light on the board with its tiny racecourse, now lying in ruins. Bernard had got angry with Yolande who was cheating shamelessly. In an instant, the little horses had gone flying to every corner of the table. Only one was left standing, a green one, on the square marked 7.

Yolande wasn't going to play with Bernard any more. She was asleep, chin on her chest, arms hanging by the sides of the chair and a mauve crocheted shawl round her shoulders. She had quickly tired of being Bernard and Yolande, switching from one side of the table to the other. After a short while she had lost track of who she was.

Then she had played the part of Bernard in a rage, simply to have done with it.

Bernard had gone off to his room in a sulk. Yolande would have liked to play on. She hated things coming to an end. She'd always been like that. She'd never wanted to get off a merry-go-round. Later on when she'd go out partying all night, she took badly to the first glimmerings of dawn. She'd get angry with the people who left her and went off to bed. When there was a biscuit she liked, she wouldn't eat just one but ten, even if it made her sick. Nothing was ever supposed to stop.

Every night she struggled against sleep. She lost every time, but one day she'd win. She would keep her eyes open, like statues do. She might be covered in moss and pigeon droppings but she would not let her eyelids close. Generations of dribbling old men and snivelling babies would pass by and she wouldn't so much as blink.

Seeing her like this, wound in her mauve shawl like a withered bouquet, you'd never know she was made of indestructible stuff. Time had been on her side since birth. Yolande was life's great witness. Let them go and get buried in their lousy cemeteries. Their marble slabs and plastic flowers would rot before she'd lost a single tooth. There was nothing they could do to her, and that's what really got to them. She was like the sea, they could throw anything they wanted at her, even an atom bomb. *Boom!* it would go, and then the surface would grow perfectly smooth again as if nothing had happened. Scarcely a ripple. And when she'd had enough of everyone swarming around, then she would overflow, in wave upon wave from her statue body. In her sleep, Yolande parted her thighs and revelled in peeing where she sat.

Yolande had awoken with a start, a silent cry filling her mouth. Something had smashed on the floor. Her bowl half full of red wine. Some creature going past, no doubt. They were everywhere. You couldn't see them but they were there, nibbling, scrabbling, gnawing even the very shadows. She pushed the shards of her bowl under the table with the toe of her slipper. Her back hurt, the chair had been pressing into her ribs. It was a horrible day. Although it had barely begun, she could sense that from a thousand tiny details, her itching head, the cold in her bones, the way things all seemed to have moved imperceptibly from their usual places so her hand had to feel around for them. The matches that needed striking ten times before she could light the gas. Yolande set the water to boil because she had to start somewhere. She pressed up against the cooker, her hands cupped round the small blue flames. She felt stiff, as rigid as the chair on which she had spent the night. Her neck and knees cracked with every movement. The water took for ever to come to the boil. Yolande poured in half a jar of instant coffee, added four or five sugar lumps and filled a cup that was as stained as an old pipe. The first scalding mouthful made her cough. Then she busied herself, moving things about for no reason, just to avoid being paralysed by the light filtering through the world's arsehole. She made heaps, heaps of little horses, heaps of biscuit crumbs, heaps of little balls of paper, heaps upon heaps, stacked up the plates with leftover food congealed on them, donned coat upon coat, and put socks on over her slippers.

She ran from one place to another, bumping into stacks of newspapers which collapsed in her wake, raising clouds of outdated information. Everywhere she felt hunted by the pale light creeping in like smoke through the gaps in the shutters, and the keyholes. All those gaps had to be plugged with scrunched-up pages of newspaper. On one of them the distressing photo of Maryse L. crumpled and disappeared in her hands. As she went to plug one last slit in a shutter, Yolande had time to see the Germans hiding on the other side of the street and a handful of Resistance fighters springing from one dustbin to the next. They no longer had enough space outside to fight their war, now they wanted to do it in her house. In her terror she found cracks in every corner, one there, another one here! The daylight was pressing with all its might against the walls. She didn't have enough arms to battle against the pressure from outside. There was cracking and banging on all sides. It was so powerful and she was so fragile. She rushed into Bernard's room. A troop of rats fled at her approach. She began to lay into her brother with her fists.

'Bastard! How can you abandon me now?'

Shaking with fury, she grabbed the cover from the bed, put it over her head and huddled down behind the door, arms wrapped tightly, so tightly round her knees, a mass of shivers. On the mattress the exposed corpse gave a toothy grin.

It was past nine at night, yet the lights were still on in the café. This was the only light in the darkness shrouding Place de la Gare. It looked like a fish tank filled with yellow oil, inside which Roland was darting back and forth, giving things a wipe down with his cloth, a bullfighter's cape without a bull; it was lovely and idiotic at the same time, as he was alone amid the tables and chairs. A car zoomed away from behind the premises. Jacqueline was at the wheel. She hadn't even taken off her apron, just put on a big woollen jacket on top. Her hair was a mess, there was anxiety in her gestures. In the rear-view mirror she glanced at her swollen right eye.

'Lousy bastard!'

She could no longer remember what had started it, something insignificant as usual, a few centimes out on a bill, a disagreement over what to watch on TV, a word out of turn. In recent months she and Roland had been sitting on a powder keg, the tiniest spark was enough to blow it all sky high. That evening they'd reached the very end of the road. It wasn't Féfé's head Bernard should have put a bullet in, but that arsehole's.

'Just take a look at yourself, with your big fat beer belly hanging out everywhere, your furred-up tongue and your bulging eyes. What a handsome footballer!'

'You're having a go at me! Have you looked in the mirror lately? You've got tits like floppy flannels and hair like a floorcloth. Even those piece of shit Arabs building the motorway wouldn't be turned on by you. You're ancient, old girl, you're ugly, and you smell of dishwater.'

'Maybe not to everyone.'

'All right, you bring that Bernard here, then, the poofter, and I'll show him a thing or two. I may not be perfect, but at least I don't rape young girls, kill women and murder kids!'

'What are you talking about?'

'I'm saying what I know. Young Maryse who's never been found, the murdered woman on the building site, all that started at precisely the time Monsieur Bernard began prowling about the area.'

'My poor Roland, you really should stop drinking, it's sad …'

'We'll see about that. And what was your precious Bernard up to beside the warehouse when the kid got himself stabbed? I saw him! I was driving past and I saw him even if he did turn away when I slowed down. What's your answer to that?'

'You're talking rubbish.'

'We'll see who's talking rubbish tomorrow when I go to the police.'

'You wouldn't do that.'

'Watch me.'

'Leave him alone. You know perfectly well he's ill.'

'Ill, my arse! He's a dirty, lousy, two-faced fucking murderer! Ill or not, he'll pay for it, just like his slag of a sister did, even if she did get off too lightly!'

'Oh that's right, when it comes to dishing out justice your family are the experts. Wasn't it your father, who'd feathered his nest on the black market, that shaved her head? Right here in this room?'

'Don't you talk about my father like that, you slut. Tomorrow I'm going to the police and I'm telling them what I know!'

'You're a hero of the Resistance too, now, I suppose. You disgust me! Anyway, you won't go, you don't have the balls.'

'So that's what you think, is it?'

His fist had caught her full in the face. She'd just had time to fling a chair at his legs before making a run for it.

'Bastard! Rotten bastard!'

And yet, though she wouldn't admit it to herself, the accusations were eating away at her like a worm in an apple. In her shocked state and at night, anything became possible, question marks dangled from the stars like fish hooks. It would be good to pull in the net and find it empty but, to be honest, Bernard had been so strange lately it was as if he had a secret, something he was keeping to himself, something which, like all secrets, was just dying to burst from his lips. But that was his illness, nothing but his illness. It was unthinkable that Roland should poison his last days by setting the police on him. That scumbag would stop at nothing. Bernard, a killer?

It's difficult to drive with only one eye, you only see half the world, the uglier half. She couldn't really remember the way to Bernard's, she'd only been there once or twice, a very long time before. A sombre, grey house – she'd had to wait outside.

'I'm sorry, Yolande's very fragile. Oh shit, my keys … It doesn't matter, I always leave a spare set under the flowerpots.'

That had been a lovely day. Roland had gone off to Le Touquet for three days, to a café owners' meeting, something she'd got out of without even having been invited. It was a Sunday, and there hadn't been many for lunch. By three o'clock she was free. Bernard had taken her to the forbidden places of their childhood. They'd both been a little tipsy, had forgotten, for a few hours, who they were. And during those few hours they'd found they were unchanged, free of the little nicks in the skin at the corners of their eyes. They'd seen the sea tumbling pebbles on the beach, and imitated the gulls, turning their scarves into wings; they'd eaten chips though they weren't hungry, drunk beer without a thirst, like any other couple trailing their Sunday behind them like an ornamental poodle. A few hours in which they could believe they were what they never would be. Roland wouldn't be back until the next day. Like misers they counted out the hours, minutes and seconds they had left. Bernard had suggested the cinema.

'Five minutes – I'll be right back.'

She had seen him hunting around under the geranium pot which contained nothing but a spadeful of dry soil, then give three knocks on the door and disappear inside after turning the key. For the twenty minutes during which she had waited in the car, she'd wondered what Yolande would look like after so long. And what it was like in their house, and what it would have been like at Bernard and Jacqueline's if life had had other ideas. She was on to the choice of wallpaper in the bedroom when he had emerged again, gaunt and looking sad.

'I'm so sorry, Jacqueline, we're going to have to call it a day. She's not well. I'll take you home.'

'I quite understand,' she'd said, strangling her scarf on her knees.

Life had had the same lurid violet tint as this evening, and the sweep of the headlamps was powerless to soften it.

'Oh where is it? Bloody hell!'

There it was, it was coming back to her now. The disused mine shaft, and the first hovels of this dump which might indeed be called 'Bloody Hell'. Her right eye felt like a piping-hot fried egg stuck to her cheek. The only light in the windows she passed was from the bluish TV screens. One more right turn, all the way along, the very last house.

Others had sprung up in the meantime but it was easy to recognise, grey, unseeing, deaf. Jacqueline parked and switched off the engine. She hesitated then caught sight of Bernard's Renault 5 squashed up against the gate like a fag end in an ashtray. A sliver of light came from the downstairs window.

A woman, even if she's in her pinny and wearing a

black eye, always tidies her hair in the rear-view mirror.

The cold was nipping at her thighs, the points of her breasts. She ran across the road the way girls run, legs going out to the sides, holding her jacket closed across her chest with both hands. Even at fifty-five and counting, a woman is still a girl. She had to push open a rotting wooden gate with a letter box nailed to it: Yolande and Bernard BONNET.

The house seemed to hate her. She would be hard put to it to say in what way, why, and how it showed this, but it hated her. Its way of puffing out its walls as she approached, and swallowing her up in its covered doorway.

Jacqueline knocked three times, louder at each turn. All she got in reply was a dull thud as if the house wasn't hollow inside, was without resonance.

'Bernard! It's me, Jacqueline! I've got to talk to you! Open up!'

The house retreated still further into itself. Jacqueline took a step backwards and flung a handful of gravel against the shutters. Nothing.

'I know someone's there. Yolande, open the door, it's important!'

Despite the bedcover over Yolande's head, the handful of gravel was like a volley of buckshot to her. Her head was still thrumming from the knocking at the door, which had dragged her from the sleep engulfing her, soft and black as soot. They were going to mount an attack, it was imminent. They would not pass by. All these years, one on top of the other, had made the walls of the house as thick as a blockhouse's. Yolande stroked her hair. They wanted to take her back to the café, to do it all over again, that was why they'd sent Jacqueline. But Bernard had made her a promise, no one could get in, no one could see. It was like Switzerland here, the war would stay outside. To ward off ill fortune she sucked the 'More than yesterday and much less than tomorrow' pendant. The gold didn't taste of anything. It wasn't worth the blood spilt for it. With a swift tug she snapped the chain and swallowed the pendant.

Jacqueline had found the key under the flowerpot. She was reluctant to use it. This house was out of bounds, but Roland would stop at nothing. He wouldn't be sober again for a week, he'd be sprawling about at the police station. She didn't believe a word of what he was saying of course, but Bernard was so weak. She wanted people to leave him in peace for what little time he had left. The key was rusty, it lay heavy in her hand like a weapon. She gave the door one last thump.

'Bernard, Yolande, I'm begging you!'

The key grated, as if unwilling to do its job. Then the door opened.

It wasn't the noise of the key in the lock that made Yolande jump but the icy draught, the breath of the outside. That shit Bernard had betrayed her. They were there! She could hear footsteps. In her head she was yelling, 'Bastard, you bastard!' She huddled still further into the corner of the room, wrapped in the bedcover, with only her eyes peeping out. She was no longer able to control the shivers rippling through her body from head to toe. Her right hand was looking for something, it didn't matter what, as long as it could be used as a weapon. A Bic biro, a Cristal, with blue ink.

Jacqueline retched as she ventured into the hall, where an infernal stench leapt out at her like a wild cat.

'Oh, good God!'

Any rubbish tip would have looked like a picnic spot compared to this house. A heap of old newspapers collapsed as she made to steady herself against the wall. A creature slipped between her legs. Stifling a cry, she felt about for a switch but thought better of it. It might look worse in the light.

'Bernard? Yolande? Don't be frightened, it's me, Jacqueline.'

She moved forward blindly, arms outstretched in front of her, towards the glimmer coming from under a door. She had only four steps to take but it seemed like several kilometres. As she moved, among the countless stale odours crowding into her nostrils, one gradually stood out, sweetish, yellow, rancid. She had never smelt it close up and yet she knew. It was in the genes. When her father had died, the same smell had filled the air outside the room she'd been forbidden to enter.

'But why can't I go in?'

'Because.'

When her father had emerged, it had been in a long box of pale oak. The wax polish had never managed to banish the smell from that room. Gingerly she pushed the door in front of her. Centimetre by centimetre her field of vision increased: the stiff bulk of a wardrobe, the corner of a chair with a cup on it, a bedside table bearing a reading lamp with its shade at an angle and … Bernard's profile, eyes and mouth open, emaciated. Her hand flew to her mouth. Tears came into her eyes.

'No! Oh God, no!'

Her foot trod on something plastic, the lid of a pen. Bernard was staring at the ceiling with a silly grin. One of his lips seemed to have been gnawed. Bernard's elbows and knees stuck up beneath the sheet. Run away as fast as she could … But that was impossible. All the mysteries were there, all the things you want to know about 'the Hereafter'. In any case, the orders from her head were no longer getting through to her limbs. It was horrible, monstrous, but it was fascinating. She stayed there in astonishment, faced with this life in which death had taken up residence. Her blood shot up and down in her veins like an elevator gone mad, then froze around her heart. She didn't hear the bedcover moving behind her. Once upon a time there lived Bernard and Jacqueline …

Yolande had pounced, gripping the biro in her fist. Pulling Jacqueline's head back by the hair she had plunged the biro into her exposed throat. The blood spurted out, spattering Bernard's cheek. Gurgling noises came from Jacqueline's mouth. Her arms were flailing. But Yolande kept her grip. Several times she struck with the pen, into her neck, her eye, five times, ten, twenty! Until that tart from the café fell like a rag doll at her feet.

'Good shot! Good shot! Good shot!!!'

While she'd been kicking the body, Yolande had lost her slipper. She looked for it under the bed. There it was, she'd found it. As she drew her head out from under the bed again, she found herself eyeball to eyeball with Jacqueline whose face, streaming with blood, was still making drowning noises. Yolande planted her lips on Jacqueline's and kissed her greedily.

'There, that's for Bernard, you little trollop.'

Wiping her mouth on her sleeve, Yolande got to her feet. Never had she felt so cold. That was the outside rushing in.

The passageway was filled with darkness. The others must be lying in wait in the bushes. That air ... that air ... She went to close the door but it was as if she were charmed by the Pied Piper. In front of the immense dark, she wavered, stretching out her hand. The night had no walls, no limits. That was frightening and enticing at the same time. Silence didn't exist, or else it was made up of a thousand tiny sounds. The wind on her face was an invitation. 'Come, Yolande, come. Here's something that has no end.' The air took hold of her under the arms, gently, tenderly, like her lovers of long ago. Scenting the air, Yolande quivered with all those good things. She ventured on to the doorstep. The night slipped under her skirt. 'Come here, Yolande, the world is yours for the taking. You've earned it, haven't you?'

'Yes, yes. I'm coming, but I can't come like this. I've got to do my make-up first.'

Jean-Claude was a sales rep in ladies' lingerie. He had just laid the horny bitch of a wife of an unemployed man, after getting her to sign an order worth 1,500 francs. He was happy. He was on his way home to Douai. At the side of the road, his headlamps picked out a woman's shape, a platinum blonde. He slowed down and drew up alongside. Second helpings, maybe?

'Can I do anything for you?'

The face which appeared in his wound-down window left him open-mouthed: the McDonald's clown, with far too much rouge, false eyelashes and a layer of cracking plaster all over the cheeks.

'Darling?'

'No, nothing, thanks.'

Jean-Claude sped off. He was to be involved in an accident three kilometres further on as he joined the motorway. The last thing he saw in this life would be the leering after-image of Yolande on his retina.

Outside, it was like being in the cavity of a wall. All that darkness, on every side. Yolande never grew tired, she could go on walking for hours. In the house, she had given the rooms names, the five-step room, the three-step room and so on, but here you could go on walking until the end of time. You didn't feel the cold when walking. It was best to always be on the move. The far-off was so intoxicating. No matter where you were going, that was always where you ended up. One, two, one, two ... Walking, that's what mattered. There were those hiking songs: '*Un kilomètre à pied, ça use, ça use ...*' That wasn't true, it didn't wear you out, not even your toes. It was arriving that wore you out. Yolande wasn't going to arrive, ever. On leaving the house, she'd turned right, taking the road that she'd used to take to the village. It was the same, and yet not the same. There were loads of different houses which hadn't been there before, ugly, pointed bungalows with dogs howling at the gate. Often, coming home from a dance, she'd taken this road. There hadn't been all those rakes on the roofs. What did they want to go raking the sky for? To grow what? The fields hadn't changed much, with their rabbits, eyes red from the headlamps, and that fine smell of fertiliser. The soil was good, it made you want to lie down in it like a trusty old bed when you're tired.

Kneeling on the verge, Yolande grasped handfuls of earth, smearing it on her face.

She got the same pleasure from it as when she buried her nose in a hunk of freshly baked bread. She flung handfuls skywards, calling out, 'Again! Again!'

At the edge of a wood, a fox watched her go on her way singing at the top of her voice, 'Robin Hood, Robin Hood …'

The Café de la Gare still had its lights on. Roland was asleep at a table, his head buried in his arms and his hunting rifle propped up against the imitation-leather banquette. He was having a dream about hunting. He had killed all the animals in the forest and was continuing his destruction with the trees, but they were refusing to fall down. Soon he would have run out of cartridges and there were still so many trees …

Yolande's path could lead nowhere else. There was only one and it led inexorably to Place de la Gare. Everything had changed: the shops, most of the houses, the lines of certain streets, the in-your-face adverts in which naked girls who looked like her cavorted, new streetlights looking like strings of sorrowful moons along the paths. And yet nothing had changed. The same familiar ennui enveloped the house fronts, cocooning the threadbare dreams of those who were asleep inside. The three kilometres she'd covered had given her a momentum which no force on earth could stop. She wasn't going anywhere, she was simply on the move, she could cross walls, rivers, slag heaps, time itself. The end of the night was always further off, receding with every step she took. Each of her strides pushed the horizon back. A cat sprang across the road in front of her. He had mistaken her for a car, she was going so fast, eyes scouring the darkness for any signs of the past. It was still there, its lines faintly visible beneath the slap-dash paintwork of the present.

'Bastards! They're trying to make me believe ... Well, I don't believe anything and I never have.'

The remains of shouts, of taunts still hung from the leafless branches of trees: 'Slut! Whore! Give your arse to a Boche, would you? Shave her head!' They were like the tatters of burst balloons. She had never been frightened. She'd known she'd be back one day, one day which would be like a night. She went by, waving like the Queen of England.

Set in the darkness, the Café de la Gare shone like a cheap piece of costume jewellery in a La Redoute catalogue. It was cheap, bargain basement even. Yolande pushed the door, perfectly naturally. It opened, producing a half-hearted chime. The man slumped over the table hadn't reacted at all. He was snoring. The glass in front of him shuddered every time he breathed. Yolande blinked, the neon lighting was oppressive, boring into her retina. There was too much electricity in this new world, electricity everywhere, as soon as she touched the edge of a table or the back of a chair. Current, current like during a storm, blue-green zigzags snaking all around her. This world had no place for her. She wasn't electric. She didn't have little lights that came on all over like that pinball machine which flashed 'Game over!' This world was a Christmas, and she wasn't invited. She no longer understood, everything had changed, the murals had turned into enormous photographs, undergrowth in which she couldn't keep track of herself. She would have liked to go home, shut herself up and no longer see. She had no reference points, even the teaspoon lying on the counter wasn't like the one she knew. She felt hemmed in by a crowd of objects whose uses she didn't know. Only the man sprawling at the table resembled something she might have been familiar with. Timidly she went and huddled up against him, placing the rifle between her knees. The chap groaned, and shifted the shoulder with Yolande's head resting on it.

'... don't, Jacqueline ... Jacque— Shit! What the hell???'

Roland had sat up with a start.

'But ...Who are you? What the hell are you doing here?'

'André?'

'I'm not André!'

He rubbed his eyes. The person speaking to him, who thought he was his father, didn't have a real face, but rather a mush of chalk and redcurrant juice brightened by two mint-green eyes.

'What do you want with me?'

'André??? Why haven't you got old like all the others?'

'I'm not André, I'm Roland …'

Before he had time to say anything else, Yolande was on her feet again, pointing the gun in his face.

'Why aren't you dead, you fat bastard? Everyone else dies – why not you?'

'You're mistaken, I'm Roland. André was my father.'

Yolande cocked the gun.

'You're a stupid bastard, André, you always were.'

'Don't! Yolande, you're Yolande!'

At the front the bullet didn't do too much damage. It was at the back that it all burst out, sending a shower of brain and bone all over the undergrowth. On the shelves, the bottles had shrunk closer together. Not a table or a chair so much as breathed. Silence reigned once more.

All of a sudden Yolande felt very weary. Her shoulder still trembled from the kick of the rifle. She flopped down on to a chair opposite what was left of Roland.

'It's a cold world out there and I'm going to make sure they know it.'

Exhausted, Yolande went to sleep.

The Panda Theory

"You've only been here for a few days but you already know loads of people. You walk into people's lives, just like that."

Gabriel is a stranger in a small Breton town.

Nobody knows where he came from or why he's here. Yet his small acts of kindness, and exceptional cooking, quickly earn him acceptance from the locals.

His new friends grow fond of Gabriel, who seems as reserved and benign as the toy panda he wins at the funfair.

But unlike Gabriel, the fluffy toy is not haunted by his past...

ISBN 978-1-9060-4042-0
£6.99 paperback

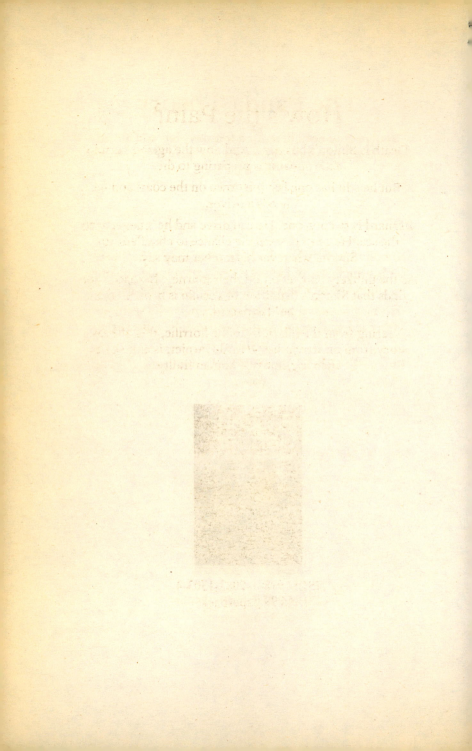

How's the Pain?

Death is Simon's business. And now the ageing vermin exterminator is preparing to die.

But he still has one last job down on the coast and he needs a driver.

Bernard is twenty-one. He can drive and he's never seen the sea. He can't pass up the chance to chauffeur for Simon, whatever his mother may say.

As the unlikely pair set off on their journey, Bernard soon finds that Simon's definition of vermin is broader than he'd expected...

Veering from the hilarious to the horrific, this offbeat story from master stylist, Pascal Garnier, is at heart an affecting study of human frailty.

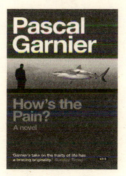

ISBN 978-1-9083-1303-4
£6.99 paperback

To be published August 2013

Moon in a Dead Eye

Given the choice, Martial would not have moved to *Les Conviviales*. But Odette loved the idea of a brand-new retirement village in the south of France.

So that was that.

At first it feels like a terrible mistake: they're the only residents and it's raining non-stop. Then three neighbours arrive, the sun comes out, and life becomes far more interesting and agreeable.

Until, that is, some gypsies set up camp just outside their gated community…

ISBN 978-1-9083-1349-2
£6.99 paperback

Pascal Garnier

Pascal Garnier was born in Paris in 1949. The prize-winning author of over sixty books, he remains a leading figure in contemporary French literature, in the tradition of Georges Simenon. He died in 2010.

Melanie Florence

Melanie Florence teaches at The University of Oxford and translates from the French.

Praise for Pascal Garnier:

'Garnier's take on the frailty of life has a bracing originality.'
Sunday Times

' ... Bleak, often funny and never predictable.'
Observer

'Action-packed and full of gallows humour.'
Sunday Telegraph

'Grimly humorous and tremendously dark ... Superb.' *Figaro Littéraire*

'Pascal Garnier is not just an accomplished stylist but also an exceptional storyteller ... *The Panda Theory* is both dazzlingly humane and heartbreakingly lucid.' *Lire*